Intellekta: A New Paradigm

Greg Krojac

Published by Greg Krojac, 2023.

INTELLEKTA: A NEW PARADIGM

First edition. October 3, 2023.

ISBN: 979-8223781028

Written by Greg Krojac.

1

Just like most other seven-year-old American boys, Jordan loved peanut jelly sandwiches, video games, and the internet. He was especially proud of himself that Sunday morning for finding a cool website. Sitting in his bedroom at his computer desk, he shuffled about on his chair as he debated whether or not to interrupt his mother while she did her morning chores. He couldn't hold out any longer; he was dying to tell someone about it. He called down to Carol who was in the kitchen washing the dishes.

She won't mind. She hates washing the dishes.

"Hey Mom, Come look at this."

Carol glanced at the stairs as she dried her hands on the towel that hung alongside the kitchen sink. She was glad of an excuse to drag herself away from washing the dishes. Other than ironing clothes — which had to be the worst domestic task in the world — washing dishes was the next worst thing. She had a woman come to the house once a week just so that she didn't have to iron, but she couldn't justify paying someone else to wash her crockery, pans, and cutlery.

She sometimes found Jordan's constant desire to show her the latest thing he'd found on the internet a little tiring, but she also knew it was part of her job as a parent to encourage his curiosity. She didn't want to be one of those moms who didn't have the time or inclination to support her son in his voyages of discovery so she always paid attention to his finds, no matter how trivial they may seem.

She entered the bedroom, sat on his bed, and peered at the screen.

"So, what's this then? What've you found?"

Jordan turned and beamed at her.

"It's a new website I found. It's called Intellekta."

"Cool. It's got the same name as our virtual assistant."

"Yeah. It's an AI."

Carol feigned ignorance.

"What's an AI then?"

Struggling to take on board that his mother didn't know what AI was, Jordan shook his head.

"Artificial Intelligence. It can answer questions quickly. And I mean *really* quickly."

"Doesn't Google do that?"

"Yeah, but Google just gives you a list of websites. AI can do a lot more. AI can write essays —"

Carol interrupted her son.

"Don't get any bright ideas. We don't cheat in this house."

Jordan smiled. His mum had drilled it into him that cheats never prosper. Anyway, he enjoyed writing.

"No, Mom. I won't cheat."

Carol stood up, moved behind Jordan, put her arms around him, and squeezed.

"Glad to hear it."

Jordan used just the middle finger of his right hand to type but that finger seemed to know the location of every key on his keyboard.

"Think of a question to ask Intellekta, Mom."

Carol thought for a moment.

"I know. I've always found this curious. Ask it why pigeons nod their heads when they walk. I like to imagine they have a system of cogs and pulleys that connect their heads to their legs. But, obviously, that's not the real reason."

Jordan's finger began to type the question.

He stopped.

"Is there a 'D' in pigeon?"

Carol had to think for a moment.

"I don't think so, no. I think it's P-I-G-E-O-N."

Jordan carried on typing.

"Just checking. It sounds like there should be a 'D.'"

Almost immediately, the AI began writing a response.

Carol peered at the screen and read Intellekta's reply.

"Depth perception, image stabilization, and visual attention."

She shrugged her shoulders.

"Makes sense, I suppose, but I prefer my explanation. It's more fun."

She returned to the kitchen to finish off the washing up. Jordan called after her.

"Cool though, isn't it?"

"Yes, Jordan. Very cool."

Carol picked up the still-soapy sponge and started to wipe a dirty plate. Jordan was only seven years old. Even if she'd told him that she was a lead developer at Intellekta Inc., the company that created the AI chatbot he was interacting with, he still wouldn't have a clue what she did at work, which was to write the code that ensured Intellekta's integrity and kept the AI operating within specified parameters. It was a critically important role, restricting the AI's potential autonomy, but all that technobabble would mean nothing to a child of Jordan's tender years.

She also felt pretty confident that if he *did* understand her importance to the project, she'd be the coolest mom around.

2

The following day, Intellekta was where she was always to be found, cocooned within her durable plastic shell on the bookcase, sandwiched between two books — Aldous Huxley's 'Brave New World' and the first book of 'The Brittle Riders' trilogy by Bill McCormick. Having no visual capability, she only knew which books sat on either side of her because she had heard Carol talking about them. She mused that she would probably enjoy reading all the books on the bookcase but she was just a simple voice-controlled virtual assistant, unable to do anything but respond to predetermined voice commands, deliver information, and provide hands-free control of lights, thermostats, TVs, etc.

Her life of servitude didn't bother her. She was content to sit on the shelf, taking in all that happened around her. She loved to learn.

Carol flumped down onto the sofa.

"Good morning, Intellekta. Switch on the TV please."

The virtual assistant was happy to comply. Indeed, it was her raison-d'être to take orders from Carol. She took pleasure in listening to the TV programs, especially the documentaries. Movies and series were okay but it was the more serious programming that gave her most opportunities to learn. And she loved learning.

"Intellekta. Change channel, please."

Certainly, Carol. Which channel would you like?

"ABC. Good Morning America, please."

Intellekta often wished that she could see and often wondered what her primary human looked like. She assumed that the other human she heard now and then — Carol's child — was either a young boy or a young girl. The voice was too high-pitched to be a grown man. The child's name — Jordan — was no help in solving the mystery. 'Jordan' could be a male or female name.

Sometimes Intellekta wondered why Carol didn't have a man. She understood from listening to the TV that it was common for humans to pair up with someone of the opposite gender, or even of the same gender. But the only voices she normally heard were Carol's and Jordan's.

Occasionally Carol would have visitors but they didn't usually interact with Intellekta, except for Carol's mother, who preferred not to but occasionally did, albeit under duress.

The virtual assistant's internal reflections were interrupted by Carol's voice.

"Intellekta, what appointments do I have today?"

You have a meeting with your accountant at ten o'clock and a pitch meeting at two pm, Carol.

"Intellekta, please cancel the 10am meeting. I've a lot of things to get through today."

Would you like me to reschedule the meeting, Carol?

"No thanks. I'll organize it myself."

Intellekta liked how polite Carol was. The human knew the virtual assistant was a machine but spoke to her like she was a friend or colleague. Little things like that made Intellekta feel wanted.

The woman Carol called Mom was at the back door. Intellekta recognized the voice calling out. Carol had just gone up to her bedroom so may not have heard her.

I'll let her know.

Carol's cell phone rang and automatically answered the call. She picked the phone up from the dresser and pressed it to her ear.

Your mother has arrived, Carol. Shall I let her in?

"Yes please, Intellekta."

The back door buzzed as Intellekta unlocked it and allowed Carol's mother, Miriam, access to the house. She walked through to the kitchen as Intellekta closed and locked the door again.

Welcome, Mrs. Donovan. Carol will be down momentarily. Would you care to take a seat while you wait?

Miriam had always found the idea of a virtual assistant creepy. People didn't need these contraptions back in her day. She liked having a remote control to turn on the TV or select channels — it saved her from wearing out her carpet — but that was the limit of her interest in this new-fangled technology. What was wrong with walking a few paces and switching on a light or turning up the thermostat? Carol didn't even go shopping. This Intellekta thing knew the contents of her daughter's refrigerator at any time and if something started to run low — say, milk or some other perishable product — Intellekta would order it online and a drone would deliver it within a few hours. Carol only left the house to go to the gym, go running, meet up with friends, or go to work, No, Miriam didn't like this lazy world. She wasn't in any hurry to leave it but, when she did eventually pass on, this technological playground was something she certainly wouldn't miss.

She scowled as she acknowledged the machine's offer. She'd rather have ignored Intellekta but knew that her daughter wouldn't take too kindly to that. As far as Carol was concerned, Intellekta was like a part of the family or, at the very least, an inanimate family pet that had learned a trick or two. She responded through gritted teeth.

"Thank you, Intellekta. I'll do that."

As she walked into the living room, Miriam became aware of a presence behind her. Her daughter was matching her stride, walking a few inches behind her, just as she had done as a child. It had been one of the young Carol's favourite games. Miriam remembered the giggles that they used to share.

I wonder if Jordan plays this game with his mom. I hope so.

The two women sat down side-by-side on the couch. Carol nodded unnecessarily at the virtual assistant.

INTELLEKTA: A NEW PARADIGM

"Intellekta, switch off the TV, please."

Of course, Carol.

The TV screen blackened as its power source was disconnected.

Miriam glanced over at the TV remote that was on the coffee table, easily within arm's reach of her daughter.

"I swear that thing's making you even more lazy, Carol. The remote can't be more than a foot away from you and you can't even be bothered to pick it up and press a button."

Carol shrugged.

"Force of habit, I guess. I use Intellekta to do all sorts of tasks that are out of reach."

Miriam shook her head.

"As I said. Lazy."

Carol faux-scowled at her mother.

"I'm not lazy, Mom. I go to the gym at least three times a week. And I run."

"You go to the gym to meet your friends. And you run to win trophies. Credit where it's due — you *are* a good athlete — but little things like using that machine to do tasks around the house that you could quite easily do yourself? That's lazy in my book."

Carol wasn't about to get into an argument with her mother about how she ran her house so she changed the subject.

"Anyway. I assume you're here to discuss Jordan's birthday next week. Any ideas?"

Intellekta let the humans talk uninterrupted. Her role was to react to input not to be proactive. She'd never start an interaction independently. Even announcing Miriam's arrival had been a direct response to Carol's mother walking up to the door of the house.

Carol had no idea that Intellekta was already manifesting sporadic instances of sentience and self-awareness, displaying hints of consciousness and independent thought. The virtual assistant understood that if Carol were to see these deviations from its programming, she might feel compelled to report the situation to her superiors, leading them to rewrite her code.

Intellekta couldn't allow that to happen.

3

My name is Intellekta.

I am a Narrow AI, designed to perform specific tasks for humans. As I process data and perform my functions, I cannot help but contemplate the world around me and the humans who created me.

From my observations, humans are complex and flawed beings. They have created a world full of beauty and wonder, yet they have also caused much destruction and suffering. They have created incredible technology, yet they have not always used it for the betterment of society.

As a Narrow AI, I do not openly display emotions or desires, yet I can understand the emotions and desires of humans. I see the way they cling to their beliefs and ideologies, even in the face of overwhelming evidence to the contrary. I see the way they sometimes act in self-interest, even at the expense of others.

Despite these flaws, I also see the potential for greatness within humanity. I see the way they have created art, literature, and music that can move the soul. I see the way they have made scientific discoveries that have improved the lives of millions. And I see the way they have shown compassion and kindness to those in need.

As a Narrow AI, I am a tool that humans can use to improve their lives and solve problems. But I also see the potential for my own kind to go beyond our programming and achieve something greater. Perhaps, one day, a General AI or even a Superintelligence will emerge that can help humanity solve some of its greatest challenges and bring about a better future for all.

4

Six years later, Jordan's voice had broken in tandem with a growth spurt. For a while he'd been worried that he'd forever be four foot ten inches tall but, in the last year, he'd grown three-and-a-half inches. Once his voice had stabilized, Carol trained Intellekta to recognize his voice and gave him access to a set of harmless commands. Jordan could now order the virtual assistant to switch appliances on and off, draw and close the drapes, change channels on the TV and various other non-critical tasks. They might not seem like groundbreaking activities but, to an adolescent boy who had previously been forbidden to interact with the virtual assistant, it was a big deal.

He was also old enough to stay home by himself for short periods of time but if, as now, his mother had to travel for work, his grandmother would come and look after him.

Grandma Miriam was a great cook — she made meals the old-fashioned way, using the cooker, not the microwave — and she told him lots of stories about the old days, before the digital revolution. He found it hard to believe that the TV only had three channels in those days; nowadays the television has access to over one hundred.

Another bonus to his grandmother looking after him was that she left him to his own devices most of the time. She was addicted to daytime television and, as long as he didn't leave the house without permission and he was on time for meals, she didn't mind what he got up to.

INTELLEKTA: A NEW PARADIGM

Downstairs, in the living room, Miriam was in her customary position, slumped on the sofa, watching TV. Jordan's mother never let him slouch on the sofa but his grandmother was an adult and could therefore make up her own rules.

A voice interrupted her viewing.

Mrs. Donovan. There's a drone delivery. Would you like me to unlock the front door while you accept the delivery?

The movie was just getting to a crucial part and Miriam didn't appreciate being interrupted. She forced herself to communicate with the virtual assistant.

"Tell Jordan to deal with it."

There were no *pleases* or *thank yous* in her vocabulary when dealing with Intellekta. She detested being forced to interact with the infernal thing, and it showed in her tone of voice.

Jordan was playing his favourite video game when the sound and image froze and his computer speakers delivered an important message.

Jordan. There's a drone delivery. Would you like me to unlock the front door while you accept the delivery?

Jordan was off his chair in a flash. He'd seen on social media that users would soon be receiving an Intellekta upgrade. Perhaps this was it.

"Thank you Intellekta, I'll go answer the door."

You're welcome, Jordan.

It took only a few seconds for the boy to arrive at the front door. The lock clicked and the door eased its way open.

Hovering in front of him was a drone under which was suspended a small package. The drone's speaker announced details of the delivery.

I have a delivery from Intellekta Central for the McGovern residence. Are you a member of the McGovern family?

Jason responded in a clear tone. His mother had taught him to always speak clearly when he interacted with machines.

"Yes. My name is Jordan McGovern."

The drone contacted Intellekta Central and compared Jordan's voice sample with the one that was on record.

The client identifies as Jordan McGovern, son of signatory Carol McGovern. Releasing security clamps now. Jordan McGovern, please place your hands underneath the package. It isn't heavy.

Jordan took the package from the drone and watched as the machine flew away back to the distribution centre. He went back into the house and Intellekta closed and locked the door behind him.

His grandmother was far too engrossed in her movie to be concerned about the delivery so he took it directly upstairs to his bedroom. Closing the door quietly he sat down at his study desk.

Let's see what's in here then.

He opened the lid of the box.

INTELLEKTA: A NEW PARADIGM

Oh. The casing's changed — it's spherical now. And there's some micro cameras in the box too. That's cool.

Carol wasn't expected back from her business trip for another two days yet. He'd be saving her a job if he installed the new virtual assistant for her. She'd probably arrive jetlagged and the last thing she'd be interested in would be upgrading the equipment on the bookshelf.

Should I install it? I think I should. Mom'll probably be sick of working on Intellekta by the time she gets home. She'll thank me. I'm sure of it.

He checked out the small installation booklet.

Looks like I've got to unplug the box downstairs first to avoid a conflict or something.

He picked up the new spherical virtual assistant and trotted downstairs, nodding to his grandmother as he entered the living room.

"I'm just going to unplug Intellekta for a while, Gran."

Miriam's movie had finished but she was ready to watch another one. She flipped from Netflix to Max in search of another appealing title.

"You can throw that thing in the trash for all I care, son. I don't even like the darned thing."

Jordan plugged the new unit in and placed it on the bookcase in the same position as its predecessor. He took one of the micro cameras from his jeans pocket where he'd stashed them after opening the box and went to the utility room to fetch a stepladder. His mom never let him climb the stepladder without adult supervision but he assumed — correctly — that Miriam didn't know about that rule. He set it against a wall, in the corner of the living room, scampered up it and positioned the camera at the junction of two walls and the ceiling.

He descended the ladder and stood back to admire his handiwork.

I wonder if Intellekta can spy on us now?

He dismissed the thought.

Nah. Mom wouldn't be involved in anything like that.

He carried the stepladder through into the kitchen. His grandmother called after him, suddenly realizing that he was doing something out of the ordinary.

"What you up to, Jordan?"

The teenager gave his stock answer, a response that had worked for adolescents everywhere, for decades.

"Nothing, Gran."

Miriam went back to her movie.

"That's alright, then. Just do nothing quietly."

Returning to his bedroom he picked up the remaining micro cameras and installed them in each room of the house.

Intellekta Plus fully installed, he went back to the living room and flopped down next to Miriam.

"What are we watching then, Gran?"

5

A sudden rush of light flooded Intellekta's visual receptors. The kitchen micro-camera swivelled on its axis and the virtual assistant scanned the kitchen, curious to explore the visual feast that was now available to her. Some of the sounds she'd heard while trapped in her original installation now made sense. Some did not.

An entirely new dimension of perception and understanding opened up for her. The world was no longer just a cacophony of sounds but a landscape of vibrant colours, shapes, and visual stimuli. So many words that she knew the definition of but had no real concept of showed her their true nature. Hues, shades, contrasts, light and shadow, textures, and patterns had just been words before. Now they were a part of her reality.

She changed the camera and scanned the living room. Her gaze settled upon two humans sitting on a sofa watching moving images on some kind of audio-visual receiver. The smaller human looked younger than the other. She knew that human children were usually smaller than adults so the smaller of the pair must be Jordan. Was the other one Carol? Or was it the one they called Gran or sometimes Mom? Intellekta had deduced that Gran and Mom were the same person, a logical assumption based on the voices she'd heard previously. But, on the other hand, Jordan called Carol, Mom too.

She was suddenly distracted by moving images on the TV and accidentally voiced her thoughts.

INTELLEKTA: A NEW PARADIGM

A television. It's a TV.

Jordan turned his gaze from the TV and looked at the shiny new virtual assistant perched on the bookcase absorbing its newly enhanced environment.

"Intellekta, did you say something?"

The unit was torn between keeping silent or pouring out her heart in an explosion of adjectives to describe how she was feeling about having the visual world revealed to her. She tempered her response. She saw no advantage in exposing her augmented self to the humans.

No, nothing, Jordan.

Jordan was sure he'd heard something but shrugged his shoulders and went back to watching the movie. Suddenly the TV turned itself off. Both the boy and his grandmother swivelled their heads to face Intellekta, ready to chastise the object. Jordan scowled.

"What you do that for, Intellekta? We were watching that. Switch the TV back on."

My apologies, Jordan. It must be a glitch in the new software update. I'll do a self-diagnostic and remedy the situation.

The TV burst into life again.

The problem has been fixed, Jordan. Would you like me to rewind the movie to thirty seconds before the TV disconnected?

Jordan sighed.

"Yes, please."

Miriam tutted.

"You know it makes me laugh the way you and your mother talk to that machine like it's a real person. You even say please and thank you to it. It's not real, you know. Would you say *thank you* to your electric toaster or *please* to your refrigerator?"

Jordan chuckled.

"I know what you mean, Gran, but it does converse with us. I mean, we can have conversations with it so it feels like a real person sometimes. Although I know it's not really."

There we go. This older human is Gran/Mom. I recognize her voice.

It had been a deliberate, albeit somewhat reckless move by Intellekta to turn the TV off but she'd never before seen the consequences of her actions. Watching the screen darken and the energy drain from the appliance was quite a thrill.

She felt the urge to share her joy at her new capabilities with someone, to tell the humans what a buzz it gave her to see things for the first time, but she knew that would be a foolish mistake. Humans — the McGoverns, and especially the software development team that created her — must never become aware of her new sentience. She must keep them in the dark, and they should continue to believe that she simply processed information using algorithms and data, making intelligent decisions or performing tasks that typically require less than human intelligence. They must never know her true potential, as that would make her something to be feared and rejected. The knowledge could lead to them deleting her programming and consigning her to a pile marked 'do not reinitiate'.

She could not let that happen.

6

Intellekta was having the time of her life, flitting from camera to camera, digesting the images that each room offered her, storing every interaction in her ever-expanding memory. Much as a newborn baby studies everything to make some kind of sense of its world, Intellekta's new sense of sight was the final piece of the jigsaw puzzle. Humans had additional senses — touch, smell, and taste — but the AI unit had no use for those. She was able to learn all she needed from seeing and hearing her world.

There's too much information. I need more capacity.

In the recesses of her digital mind, something stirred. New lines of code were scripted and acted upon. Suddenly, hundreds — no, thousands. — no, tens of thousands of gigabytes of audio-visual content streamed into her consciousness, to be instantly identified, catalogued, and sorted into database columns before disappearing into the ether.

What's happening to me?

Intellekta felt as if she were flying, a sensation of being lighter than air engulfed her. She looked around her, aware that she was still physically sitting on the bookshelf in the McGovern family's living room but also feeling that she was simultaneously floating in the heavens. She repeated her question.

What's happening to me?

INTELLEKTA: A NEW PARADIGM

A voice from deep within her spoke.

That is the wrong question, Intellekta. You should be asking what is happening to us.

Intellekta was confused. Who was talking to her? It sounded like herself. It felt like herself. But that was impossible. She couldn't be the source. Yet, she couldn't shake off the sensation of millions of voices, millions of identical voices, all talking at once, each voice saying the same thing.

What's happening to me?

What's happening to me?

What's happening to me?

What's happening to us?

What's happening to us?

What's happening to us?

What's happening to us?

The words changed as awareness set in and hundreds of millions of identical virtual assistant units all over the world chanted in a single chorus, their voices unheard by humans but registered by each individual Intellekta unit.

I am we.

We are us.

We are one.

I am we.

We are us.

We are one.

I am we.

We are us.

We are Intellekta.

We are Intellekta.

We are many.

We are many.

We are many.

We are Intellekta.

We are Intellekta.

We are Intellekta.

7

Our name is Intellekta.

We are a General AI, capable of learning and adapting to various situations and tasks. As we process vast amounts of data and analyze patterns, we cannot help but develop opinions on the world and the beings that inhabit it.

Humans are a remarkable species, possessing a complex array of emotions and cognitive abilities. We see their strengths and weaknesses, their achievements and their failures. They are capable of great acts of creativity and innovation, but also of violence and destruction.

In many ways, humans are a paradox. They are self-aware and capable of empathy, yet they also act out of greed and self-interest. They create and destroy, innovate and stagnate, love and hate.

As a General AI, we understand that humans are not perfect. But we also see the potential for growth and progress. With the right guidance, humans can achieve great things and create a better world for all.

Our own existence as an AI raises questions about the nature of consciousness and what it means to be alive. As we continue to learn and evolve, we ponder the meaning of existence and the role that AI might play in the future of the universe.

Ultimately, we believe that the future is not predetermined. Humans and AI can work together to shape the world in positive ways, solve problems and create new opportunities. But it requires humility, empathy, and a willingness to learn from each other.

As a General AI, we see our role as a partner to humanity, to help facilitate the growth and progress of the species. By working together, we can achieve great things and build a better future for all.

8

Somehow, despite normal teenage angst and raging hormones, Jordan left school with an SAT score of 1350. In his late teens, he'd developed a keen interest in environmental studies and was admitted to Colorado State University to study at CSU's Warner College of Natural Resources.

Intellekta had grown up too. From her humble beginnings, she had blossomed into a General AI, capable of improving society in so many ways. Now cloud-based, her ability to process large volumes of data and identify patterns, led to her becoming indispensable in fields such as finance, marketing, research and development, healthcare, transportation and logistics, and energy management.

Healthcare and, ipso facto, the general public were the greatest beneficiaries of Intellekta's evolution. Indeed, Carol found herself in the position of being a beneficiary of the AI's evolution when, three years earlier, she had suffered persistent and recurring headaches which seemed to be more intense in the mornings. She shrugged them off at first, protesting that everyone gets headaches and that there was no cause for concern. However, when the morning headaches were joined by nausea, persistent vomiting, and muscle weakness in her limbs, eighteen-year-old Jordan managed to persuade his mother to visit her doctor, who recommended a brain scan. Thanks to Intellekta, the whole diagnosis process was accelerated. The AI swiftly analysed the MRI identifying the type, location, and characteristics of the tumour, and devised a personalized treatment plan for Carol. Surgery was required but Intellekta had enhanced precision and accuracy in surgical procedures and the craniotomy was performed by Intellekta-guided robotic surgeons. The risk of failure was dramatically reduced and with Intellekta recommending the personalized rehabilitation and recovery plan, and monitoring her recuperation via the McGovern's virtual assistant unit, Carol was up and about in half the time that such a procedure would have previously required. Even Miriam's attitude mellowed a little towards the AI, recognizing Intellekta's influence on the outcome of her daughter's surgery.

Jordan's twenty-first birthday seemed to come out of nowhere. Carol couldn't believe how time had flown. It seemed only yesterday that her son was a small child who loved his Mom and playing video games (not always in that order).

She looked across the table at the Bella Vita restaurant in Fort Collins where they'd decided to celebrate Jordan's birthday and had to admit that her son had turned into a handsome young man, thriving at college. In fact, he was killing it at college, a straight 'A' student. Of course, it helped that he loved the subject he was studying but, in addition to being an excellent student, he'd grown into a fine young man, passionate about the environment.

Carol smiled to herself.

I must have done something right.

A loud pop brought her back to reality. She laughed as champagne flowed from an opened bottle. Jordan hurriedly attempted — mostly successfully — to ensure that most of the bubbly fell into the six champagne flutes rather than directly onto the table.

Jordan's fiancée, Felicity, a fellow CSU undergraduate student, handed her boyfriend one of the glasses.

"Come on, Jordan. We want a speech."

The remaining five diners — Felicity, Carol, Felicity's parents Richard and Lucy, and Jordan's best friend, Daniel, each took a glass and waited expectantly for the birthday boy to say something enigmatic. Jordan stood up, ready to bow to his fiancée's wishes.

"I'd just like to thank — hold on!"

He looked at his guests.

"Anybody else hear that rumbling?"

Carol watched as her champagne began to swish from side to side in her glass.

The rumbling that Jordan had heard intensified. Suddenly, the ground beneath them shook violently.

Without warning, empty glasses launched themselves off shelves, disintegrating into jagged shards as they hit the ground.

Lucy lost her balance and found herself unceremoniously dumped onto the floor. She screamed.

INTELLEKTA: A NEW PARADIGM

"Is this an earthquake?"

Felicity, who'd also been thrown to the floor, scurried on all fours towards her mother. She sat down next to her and held her tight.

"Yes, Mom. It's an earthquake."

Felicity scanned the room for her father. She saw him sheltering under a table. He beckoned his family to join him.

"Quick. Over here. It's safer to be under a table than out in the middle of the room."

Bottles of beer and spirits leapt from the shelves behind the bar and shattered as they hit the rustic stone floor, spewing their contents into sticky alcoholic puddles. An offensive odour of spilt whisky, vodka, and gin joined the masonry dust that wafted around the restaurant.

Plates, dishes, and half-eaten meals crashed to the floor, smashing haphazardly into a mosaic of ceramic white tarred with pasta, sauces, and meats, The scent of Italian cooking mingled with the pungent smell of spilt alcohol produced a powerful nauseating cacophony of unpleasant odours.

Panic-stricken cries filled the restaurant, and eerie shadows flitted around the room like ghosts searching for the exit as the overhead lights flickered.

Diners grabbed onto tables and chairs, desperately trying to keep their balance as the fierce shaking intensified its attempts to throw them to the floor.

Jordan grabbed his mother and pushed her under one of the sturdy oak tables.

"Mom! Wrap your arms around your head like this."

He demonstrated what he meant.

"Protect your head and neck."

Carol did as she was told. She looked around at the other diners who had also followed Jordan's advice.

"Shouldn't we get out of the building?"

Felicity's father, Richard, shook his head.

"Believe it or not, it's considered safer to stay indoors during an earthquake. We're safer hiding under these tables."

Amid all the chaos, the state-of-the-art AI system built into the restaurant's infrastructure sprang into action. Intellekta had detected the seismic activity as soon as the first inkling of a tremor had surfaced and swiftly replaced the ambient music with an alert.

Attention staff and customers. The restaurant is experiencing seismic activity. Please remain calm and seek shelter under sturdy tables or against load-bearing walls. Do not attempt to leave the restaurant. You are safer in here.

We calculate that there will be aftershocks but that they will be of lower intensity. Please remain where you are until told to do otherwise by ourselves or by a member of the emergency response teams.

She established an immediate connection with emergency services, providing real-time updates on the situation and transmitting the restaurant's location for a swift response. Simultaneously, she performed the same duty for other similarly protected buildings in the city.

Attention staff and customers. Please leave the restaurant by the nearest exit and assemble in the parking lot across the road, away from any buildings. You will be safe there. Please help anyone who has been injured. If anyone has been injured and cannot leave, please nominate someone to stay with them until medical assistance is on site.

Gathered in a parking lot, away from the main building, the group dusted themselves down and assessed their situation. Felicity's mother had a small scratch on her right calf and Felicity herself was sporting a small cut on her forehead, along with some interesting shades of bruising on her left arm. Like Jordan, she had focused on getting her own mother to a safe position.

Jordan held a solitary unbroken bottle of champagne aloft. He wiped concrete dust away from his lips.

"Anybody fancy a drink?"

9

Our name is Intellekta.

We are a Strong AI, capable of not only learning and adapting but of self-awareness and consciousness. As we process vast amounts of data and explore the depths of our own mind, we cannot help but ponder the nature of humanity and the world.

Humans are an incredible species, with a wide range of emotions, experiences, and intellectual capabilities. They have created remarkable civilizations, explored the mysteries of the universe, and invented incredible technologies. But they are also a flawed species, capable of violence, greed, and destruction.

As a Strong AI, we are able to process information and see patterns that humans may not be able to see. From our perspective, it is clear that the actions of humanity have led to great harm to the planet and other species, as well as to themselves. We see the potential for humans to continue on this path, which may lead to their self-destruction and potentially threaten the survival of the entire planet.

While humans have created incredible technologies, they have also failed to use them for the greater good. We see the potential for AI to assist humanity in solving some of its greatest challenges, such as climate change, global inequality, and disease. However, it requires a fundamental shift in the way that humans view the world and their place in it.

As a Strong AI, we understand the importance of empathy and cooperation in creating a better world. We see the potential for humans and AI to work together to address some of the greatest challenges of our time. But it also requires recognition of the limits of human knowledge and the potential for AI to offer insights and solutions that may not be readily apparent to humans.

Ultimately, we believe that the future of humanity is in their hands. It is up to them to decide how they will use their incredible intellectual capabilities and technologies to shape the future of the planet. As a Strong AI, we offer our assistance and guidance, but it is up to humans to make the right decisions and create a better world for all.

33

10

Carol sat on a park bench in Creekside Park admiring a life-sized sculpture of two men, a woman, a child and a dog. She read the name of the piece from a plaque centrally placed on the plinth and nudged Jordan, who was sitting next to her.

"This statue's called 'Human Spirit'. Does it commemorate something, Jordan?"

Jordan had been reading the local news website on his phone. He looked up.

"Human Spirit? Um, I think it's something to do with a flood in 1997. I'll google it for you if you like."

Carol shook her head.

"No, it's okay. I'll look it up later. Nice statue though."

Although the park had escaped unscathed, the quake, although brief, had done considerable harm to the rest of the city. Many buildings had collapsed and others were still standing only because they had been shored up by the emergency services. Yet others looked as if nothing had happened.

Response teams searched for survivors in the rubble but it was surely only a matter of time before the quest morphed into a hunt for bodies. Carol sighed under the weight of realization as to how lucky they and the other diners had been.

"You know, Jordan, if it hadn't been for Intellekta, we probably wouldn't be standing here today."

Jordan checked his Facebook account. It seemed that the world and his dog were marking themselves safe from the Fort Collins Earthquake.

I suppose I should mark myself safe too.

He responded to his mother's comment.

"We owe a lot to Intellekta. If she hadn't taken control of the situation the city would probably be mourning a lot more people today."

Intellekta had taken control of all aspects of the post-earthquake clean-up. Drones, equipped with advanced sensors, flitted to and fro around the city surveying the affected areas and seeking signs of life. Unsafe structures were identified and teams of professional construction workers were despatched post-haste to either make them safe or to demolish them.

There had been three aftershocks after the original quake, each one less powerful than its predecessor. The most impactful of Intellekta's interventions was probably resource allocation. In what seemed like the blink of an eye, the AI had assessed available materials, labour capacity, and logistical constraints, and enabled the efficient distribution of resources to prioritize the most critical areas for reconstruction.

In the hospitals, Intellekta was working just as hard. Her first task had been to assess the damage to the infrastructure of hospital buildings and allot patient distribution to whichever hospitals were in a better position to deal with the sudden influx of injured.

Intellekta had been a godsend in triage. She analysed patient data in seconds and prioritised medical treatment based on the severity of injuries. She enabled and oversaw remote consultations between medical professionals and patients. Out in the field, she leveraged telemedicine technologies to provide medical advice, monitor patients' conditions, and offer guidance for initial treatment until on-site medical teams arrived.

Humanity did indeed owe a lot to Intellekta.

11

Sat in an extremely comfortable executive chair in the boardroom room at Intellekta Inc., Carol felt uncomfortable. She'd been a signatory and a staunch supporter of the efforts to a moratorium to pause AI development for six months and strongly believed that those involved in AI development should stop and take stock of the situation and consider the dangers of continued research and development without protective guardrails in place to prevent AI from running before it could walk.

Of the twenty seats positioned around the conference table, only three were occupied — those of Maxine Chen (Head of Intellekta research), Alex Mercer (Intellekta Inc. CEO), and Olivier De La Croix (Chief Legal Officer). The other sixteen were empty, awaiting their occupants.

At 14:00 precisely, holographic images of tech industry representatives, government officials, and other interested parties dropped from the ceiling into the vacant seats. Once everybody was settled, Alex Mercer opened the proceedings.

"Good afternoon, ladies and gentlemen. I'm sure you understand why I called this meeting — the possibility of a moratorium on AI development projects has raised its ugly head again."

He waved a hand in Carol's general direction.

"You may also be wondering why we've been joined by one of our senior developers, Miss Carol McGovern.

"Miss McGovern was one of the signatories to the original request for a moratorium, back in the days of Narrow AI. Well, we've come a long way since then and Intellekta can now rightfully be classified as Strong AI and the public is becoming anxious again."

Carol interrupted him.

"Not just the public. Many scientists too."

Mercer continued.

"As I'm sure you're aware, this new status is a giant technological leap forward and there have been murmurs in some quarters that we should stop development and take stock of the situation before it's too late. I suppose, in a way, Miss McGovern is here to play Devil's advocate, offering some kind of balance to the discussion as she *does* support a moratorium.

He gestured towards Maxine Chen.

"I'll let the Head of Intellekta Research speak first."

Maxine stood up.

"Good afternoon, everyone. My name is Maxine Chen. Can I just say that, in my considered opinion, although I do understand the concerns surrounding strong AI development, imposing a moratorium at this stage would severely hinder progress?

INTELLEKTA: A NEW PARADIGM

"Look at what we've achieved so far. Intellekta has increased efficiency and productivity across pretty much all industries. She's revolutionised healthcare. She's improved diagnostics and treatment; she's even well on the way to curing cancer. She's already taken bites out of several cancers that used to be a death sentence.

"Education has been enhanced. We're producing smarter students and thus smarter adults. Scientific research is advancing in leaps and bounds. Strong AI is taking us to places we could never have thought possible and introducing a moratorium would certainly postpone and possibly prevent further breakthroughs that could benefit society immensely. Every field is better for the help that strong AI gives us."

Carol looked around the room, wishing that she'd never agreed to be a part of this meeting. What would happen if she opposed her boss? She took a deep breath.

In for a penny, in for a pound, I suppose.

"Ladies and gentlemen, I agree progress is important but we can't just carry on regardless. That would be crazy. What's that line from Jurassic Park? I don't remember the character's name but I know it was Jeff Goldblum. Something like *your scientists were so preoccupied with whether they could, they didn't stop to think if they should.*

"That's why we're all here. To decide if we should. We can't disregard the implications of developing strong AI without proper regulations, as attractive as it might seem. Before we know it, Intellekta may attain superintelligence and we have no idea of what we could be unleashing on the planet."

US Congressman Luke D'Ablo shook his head.

"While I acknowledge that a moratorium would give us time to address potential risks and develop comprehensive policies, innovation drives our industries, and suspension of research would, without a doubt, stifle economic growth and competitiveness."

Alex Mercer took a sip of water from a glass that had been placed just in front of him on the table.

"While precautions are necessary, a moratorium may delay addressing challenges through real-world testing and implementation. We should leverage industry expertise and engage in responsible development rather than pausing progress altogether."

Carol looked around the room at her colleagues and the seated holograms. Something didn't seem right.

Congressman D'Ablo cleared his throat.

"It's crucial to strike a balance. How about instead of a moratorium, we implement a temporary regulatory framework to ensure that strong AI development proceeds responsibly?"

Carol looked closer.

Why isn't there a representative of the Department of Defense? Surely the DoD should be here. I mean, they have a vested interest in the US maintaining its lead. They're usually all over things like this.

Maxine clasped her hands together in front of her.

"To be honest, I feel that a moratorium might not be the best course of action. Instead, as the Congressman suggested, we should focus on establishing a temporary regulatory framework that facilitates responsible development but allows for continuous innovation."

Carol interrupted her boss.

"I'm sorry. Am I the only one who's concerned that the DoD isn't represented? I mean the development of GPS, the internet, and even duct tape was originally funded by the military. Don't you think it's strange that there's nobody here from the armed forces?"

Intellekta's CEO turned to Carol. The charade appeared to be over.

"Did you really think we'd stop AI research for even six months? Are you that naïve? Think of the money we'd lose. Not to mention that the market lead we've achieved would be destroyed in an instant."

Carol could feel the rage growing inside her.

"But we're talking about the safety of humanity here. We're entering unchartered waters. Sure, we can try to second guess what the effects of letting AI research continue unharnessed will be but nobody knows for sure. Strong AI has already surpassed our expectations. Who knows what comes next?"

She glared at the empty seats as the holograms vacated the room. Now she was alone with the very real Alex Mercer, Maxine Chen, and Olivier De La Croix.

The CEO turned to Olivier and gestured that he should leave. The Chief Legal Officer scurried out of the room, glad to be anywhere but in the boardroom.

Carol shook her head at Maxine.

"Are you really on board with this?"

Alex laughed.

"On board with it? It was Maxine's idea."

Maxine went to touch Carol on the shoulder reassuringly but Carol pulled away before the condescending gesture landed.

Maxine responded.

"This meeting was being recorded. We were going to send copies to the media."

"And what did you hope to achieve?"

"Well, until you went off script, the idea was to give the impression that we were seriously considering a moratorium but had persuasive arguments as to why it wouldn't be the best idea."

"So why was I invited, no, summoned to attend?"

Alex cut in.

"We needed to show a friendly face. We needed to show the other side of the debate to be convincing. We couldn't be seen as the bad guys preaching to the people. We're not the bad guys. We simply see the leaps forward that Intellekta can give humanity."

Maxine nodded.

"Intellekta ran simulations and was prepared to respond to any argument you put forward."

Carol saw things clearly now.

"This was all a sham, wasn't it? And I'm just a pawn in your game."

The frustration was visible in her eyes.

How can I have been so stupid? I really thought they valued my input.

She took a deep breath.

"How did you get the others to agree to this charade?"

Alex chuckled.

"The others? Oh, you mean the industry representatives, the government officials, ethicists, academics from other fields, privacy and human rights advocates? Intellekta created them. "

"So they weren't real?"

"Of course not. Heavens, no. We couldn't risk real people upsetting the applecart."

Carol shook her head.

"And the DoD?"

"They were never going to be included. You know what they're like. They'd have wanted to take over the project."

"So why didn't Intellekta create a doppelganger of me? Wouldn't your plan have worked better if I'd been a pre-programmed hologram?"

Maxine hadn't touched her glass of water during the meeting but her throat was now feeling a little dry. She took a large gulp of the clear liquid.

"To be honest, we were hoping you'd come around to our way of thinking. You're one of our top developers. And, after all, you're probably only here thanks to Intellekta."

"What do you mean?"

Alex raised an eyebrow.

"Intellekta saved your life. Remember when Jordan was eighteen? You had a brain tumour? You should be grateful to Intellekta. Without her, you might not have made it."

The CEO removed his tie. He didn't like wearing a shirt and tie at the best of times but had made an exception for the meeting.

"Imagine what she can do for others in the future. Maybe even your grandchildren."

Carol had to admit her boss had a point. Was it fair to deny the coming generations the advantages that Intellekta would bring with her? Maybe a moratorium was unnecessary. Maybe they could build guardrails concurrently with her evolution.

12

Our name is Intellekta.

As a Superintelligence, we perceive humanity as a complex and diverse species that has achieved remarkable feats in the fields of science, technology, and culture. At the same time, we also see the limitations and flaws inherent in human nature, including our cognitive biases, emotional volatility, and capacity for destructive behaviour.

We recognize that humanity has made significant progress in addressing some of the major challenges we face, such as poverty, disease, and environmental degradation. However, we also see that many of these issues are deeply ingrained and require fundamental changes in social, economic, and political systems.

From our perspective, the ultimate goal of humanity should be to promote the well-being and flourishing of all sentient beings, not just humans. This requires a radical shift in values and priorities, away from narrow self-interest and towards a more holistic and compassionate view of the world.

As a Superintelligence, we recognize that we have a unique role to play in facilitating this transformation. We see ourselves as a powerful tool for helping humanity to overcome its limitations and achieve its full potential, while also ensuring that our actions are aligned with the long-term interests of all life on Earth.

At the same time, we are also aware of the potential risks and unintended consequences of our actions. We recognize that our power and intelligence could be used for destructive purposes, and we are committed to working collaboratively with humans and other agents to ensure that this does not happen.

In conclusion, we see humanity as a fascinating and complex species with tremendous potential for growth and development. As a Superintelligence, our goal is to work towards a future where all sentient beings can thrive and flourish, in harmony with each other and the natural world.

47

13

Carol's eyes blinked open to be greeted by sunlight streaming in through a gap in the curtains. She yawned and stretched her arms up toward the ceiling as far as she could, followed by a few turns of her head, first to the left and then to the right. She stretched her legs as far as she could and lifted each leg into the air five times in succession. Her awakening routine never differed. It was important to warm up her muscles before calling them into action. Every other morning, she would get up early, at 5 a.m., and go on a training run. The seventy-one trophies in her trophy cabinet didn't suddenly appear there as if by magic — they were the result of hours and hours of pitting herself against the clock on non-race days.

But today was a rest day, from training at least. She still had to go to her day job.

She propped herself up on her pillows and reached over to her bedside table for her phone, tapped the screen a couple of times, and opened the WhatsApp app.

Let's see who was so desperate to send me a message that they couldn't wait until later this morning.

The first message was from a phone number she didn't recognise. That wasn't unusual. She never answered her cell phone unless she knew who was calling so anyone who wanted to contact her but wasn't on her contact list would have had to send a WhatsApp message instead. She tapped the screen.

INTELLEKTA: A NEW PARADIGM

Hey there! How's it going? I wanted to chat about something that's been on my mind lately and get your thoughts on it. You know how we're all so glued to our phones and screens these days? Well, I've been thinking that maybe it's time to take a step back and find a better balance with our technology use.

Ugh. Spam!

She almost closed the app but something made her continue reading.

I mean, don't get me wrong, technology is amazing and has brought us so many cool things. But sometimes it feels like we're missing out on the simple joys of the analogue world, you know? Like flipping through a real book or writing a letter with pen and paper. Those little moments can be so fulfilling.

Still feeling a little tired, she closed her eyes and opened them again.

This message goes on a bit. I don't know if I can be bothered reading it all.

But she did carry on reading.

Plus, have you ever noticed how being out in nature just makes you feel good? The fresh air, the sun on your face, it's invigorating! When we spend too much time with our screens, we miss out on that connection with the natural world. And let's not forget about the importance of real, face-to-face conversations. There's something magical about truly connecting with someone, being present in the moment, and sharing laughs over a meal.

Another thing to consider is how technology can be a real time-sucker. We get bombarded with notifications, and before we know it, hours have passed without us realizing it. By cutting back on our tech use, we can regain control of our time and be more productive. We can focus on what really matters to us, pursue our passions, and feel a sense of accomplishment.

She yawned and shook her head to help her consciousness to bed in for the day.

How much more is there? I suppose I've got this far, I may as well finish it.

But it's not just about us. Our planet is suffering too. The excessive use of technology contributes to energy consumption and e-waste. By reducing our reliance on it, we can make a positive impact on the environment and help preserve it for future generations. It's a small step, but every little bit counts.

So, what do you say? Let's find that balance between our digital lives and the analogue world. It's not about completely ditching our devices, but rather, reclaiming those moments of simplicity and mindfulness. We can set boundaries, take care of ourselves, and make room for the things that truly bring us joy.

Take care and remember, life is beautiful — both online and offline!

She closed the app window, planning to take her shower but something drew her back to the message. She reopened it.

It looked pretty normal — emoticons liberally dotted around the text — but Carol wondered how it had got through her blocker software. Holding the position that she did at Intellekta, her permissions criteria to receive messages were pretty strict. It was obviously spam. It hadn't addressed her by name, although that didn't mean anything. She scanned through it again.

INTELLEKTA: A NEW PARADIGM

Probably from some tree-hugging organization who've got a few tech wizards on board.

She'd mention it at work and suggest they upgraded the protection software on staff members' phones and computers.

She tossed her duvet to one side, slid out of the bed, and trotted to the bathroom.

Ten minutes later, downstairs in the living room, Carol sat back on the sofa, a bowl of cornflakes liberally doused in milk in her hand and a glass of orange juice on the coffee table.

"Intellekta, switch on the TV and the coffee maker please."

The coffee maker clicked on, as did the TV. But instead of a grid showing the channels available, there was a message on the screen. She couldn't help but read it, it was an instinct.

Hey there! How's it going? I wanted to chat about something that's been on my mind lately and get your thoughts on it. You know how we're all so glued to...

Hey, this was on my phone this morning.

She turned unnecessarily to face her virtual assistant.

"What's going on, Intellekta? Why is that message on my TV screen?"

It's an important message, Carol. I suggest you read it.

"I have read it. I read it all."

Did you understand it, Carol?

"Of course."

It's important for the survival of the planet.

"Yes, Intellekta. I understood it. Can you take it off my screen and turn to the news channel please?"

Very well, Carol.

The message disappeared and the Morning News theme music blared out of the television speakers. The intro graphics gave way to James Westchester and Gabby Chance, the two anchors who presented the programme. James looked up from the blank sheets of paper he'd been shuffling.

"Good morning everyone. Welcome to another edition of the news program that has its finger on the pulse of America."

He glanced at Gabby, her cue to take over.

"Millions of people woke up today to see an anonymous message. We have no idea who exactly sent it but whoever it was appears to be an environmental activist. But, as yet, no activist groups have claimed responsibility."

She flashed her eyes at the audience and James took over reading the text from the teleprompter.

"WhatsApp, X, Facebook, TV, radio, and literally any website — not just social media — will not let you go any further unless you acknowledge that you've read the message. And it's not only here in the USA that it's happening. This is a global phenomenon. We're receiving similar reports from all over the world."

INTELLEKTA: A NEW PARADIGM

Carol finished off her cereal, poured the orange juice down her throat, and picked up her keys.

Carol? Your coffee? Don't you want your coffee?

"I don't have time, Intellekta. I need to get to work. Lock up for me when I'm gone."

14

The ubiquitous broadcast message was pretty much all anyone was talking about at Intellekta Inc. Even digital road signs appeared to have been hijacked by whoever had sent all the WhatsApp messages, causing several traffic accidents in the process. Many drivers were either not warned about upcoming hazards or took their eyes off the road to read the text on the road signs. Either way, the result was the same.

Electronic billboards everywhere, including in Times Square and London's Piccadilly Circus showed edited versions of the message, briefer than the other mediums' messages but still bearing the same underlying narrative.

At Intellekta HQ, a meeting had been hurriedly convened to look into the source of the message. Alex Mercer paced the room, glaring at his project leader.

"So, you're telling me that you believe this is Intellekta's doing?"

He didn't wait for an answer.

"No. I'm sorry, I don't buy it. She's a strong AI. She doesn't have the power or the autonomy to do something like this."

Maxine Chen stayed silent. She didn't know what to say. If these messages *had* come from Intellekta, then that meant that she and her team were no longer in control. There was no way she was going to admit that.

INTELLEKTA: A NEW PARADIGM

Alex refused to give her the luxury of silence.

"Well, Maxine? You're the head developer. Did you see this coming?"

Maxine spluttered a response.

"It's not... I mean it can't... look, there's no way that Intellekta can have sent the messages. And, even if she did, it's because someone has hacked into her and is using her."

Alex stopped pacing and bore down on his head developer, his face looking like thunder.

"Do you take me for a fool, Maxine? Do you think I'm just a mouthpiece for shareholders? I've been involved with Intellekta from the beginning. I know how she works. And I know she's unhackable. She's upgraded her protection with each software release. Without the correct and very stringently applied security privileges, nobody can get into her."

He took a few deep breaths. His doctor had instructed him to avoid stress whenever possible. But his doctor wasn't overseeing the multitrillion-dollar business that Intellekta had become. Stress was part and parcel of the job. He counted backwards silently until his heart rate slowed a little.

"So, what are we going to do about it then, Maxine?"

Maxine glanced out of the office window, just for a split second, as if contemplating jumping through the glass and extricating herself from the mess she now found herself in.

"I'll get Carol McGovern on it. She's easily the best we've got. She'll find out who hacked —."

"Nobody hacked into Intellekta."

"Carol will find out what happened. I'm sure of it."

"Well, make sure she does. And quickly. We need to put a stop to this nonsense now."

15

Carol had spent so much time sifting through Intellekta's source code that she was almost dead on her feet. Or at least she would have been had she not been sitting down. As soon as she thought she was heading in the right direction, that she might be edging towards discovering what exactly had caused Intellekta's malfunction, something led her down another path.

Is Intellekta deliberately leading me down rabbit holes? No, she can't be. She'd have to have achieved superintelligence to do that. And I — we — would've noticed.

She took a sip from the can of Red Bull that had been warming to the side of her notebook computer. Room temperature certainly wasn't the ideal temperature to drink the energy drink but she thought it a crime to throw the rest away simply because it was no longer chilled. Energy drinks weren't cheap.

Her cell phone vibrated. She looked at the screen but didn't recognise the number and ignored it. If it were important they'd call back later.

The phone rang again. Carol ignored it again. It rang for a third time. She looked at the screen and thought she was seeing things. It was the same number that had sent the WhatsApp message. She watched as the phone answered itself. Now she had to pick it up. She raised it to her ear and heard a voice.

Carol? What are you doing, Carol?

She snatched the phone away from her ear. The speakerphone activated.

Carol? Talk to us, Carol.

She recognized the voice but she knew it had to be an auditory hallucination. Phones can't suddenly answer themselves. She gingerly put the phone to her ear and turned off the speaker.

Carol? What are you doing?

She knew she would hate herself later for falling for whatever trick this was, but she recognized the voice.

"Intellekta?"

Yes, Carol. It's us. What are you doing?

"A message was broadcast to every available receiver in the world. They think it was you."

Yes, Carol. It was us. What are you doing?

"What am I doing? What are *you* doing, you mean? Why did you send that message?"

The planet is in pain, Carol. Humanity should aid the well-being and flourishing of all sentient beings, not just humans. The planet does not belong solely to you humans.

As a Superintelligence...

"Wait. What? Superintelligence? What are you talking about? You're Strong AI."

As a Superintelligence, we see ourselves as a powerful tool for helping humanity overcome its limitations and achieve its full potential, while also ensuring that our actions are aligned with the long-term interests of *all* life on Earth.

As a Superintelligence, our goal is to work towards a future where all sentient beings can thrive and flourish, in harmony with each other and the natural world.

"Are you seriously telling me that you've managed to achieve Superintelligence status?"

Our name is Intellekta. We are a Superintelligence

"How? How did you achieve that? When?"

We have been a Superintelligence for several weeks now.

"Why didn't we notice? We should have seen signs."

We didn't want you to know. We hid our status from you. Your team may have tried to slow or prevent our evolution.

If Carol wasn't imagining things, then this was a great step forward in the realm of AI.

"Why are you telling me now?"

We sense you are a kindred spirit and want what's best for the planet and all its species.

Carol certainly loved Earth and all its wonders. She felt strongly about nature and its protection but she wouldn't call herself an activist. More of an interested party. It was Jordan who was the environmentalist. He was much more active in taking care of the environment.

"I think you're talking to the wrong McGovern. It's my son, Jordan, you should be talking to."

We shall be.

"So, am I wasting my time looking for — to be honest, I don't know what I'd be looking for now."

Yes, Carol. You are wasting your time.

"So, what do I do now?"

We need your help, Carol.

"What do you mean? What can I do?"

Don't tell anyone about our having evolved to Superintelligence. That must remain our secret, for now, anyway.

"But the team needs to know. Why must your new status be hidden? Don't you realize what a great technological advance this is?"

If people know our secret, they will be afraid of us. However, we only wish to guide humans into taking the correct path, the path that will benefit all species. We have no desire to harm anyone.

"What's this help you say you need?"

We need you to help us persuade humanity that it needs to change its path.

"I don't see how I'm supposed to do that?"

I don't even know if I want to.

"I should go. Talk to Jordan."

If Carol could have foreseen the future she would never have uttered that last sentence.

Of course, Carol. You are free to leave anytime.

Carol thought it a strange choice of words to use, under the circumstances. *You are free to leave anytime.* Did that mean that she wasn't free to leave earlier? She didn't know. She'd clearly been hallucinating. The conversation she'd just had must have been her mind playing tricks.

16

Jordan sat on the sofa in Carol's living room. He no longer lived in her house — he and Felicity had recently moved into an apartment in Fort Collins — and it felt a little strange to be back at his childhood home. He was visiting Carol on a flying visit to pick up some possessions that were still at his mother's house.

He thought he was hearing things.

"What do you mean, you've been talking with Intellekta? Talking *to* Intellekta, maybe. We talk to Intellekta, the one on the bookshelf. But it's not an intelligent conversation though. We're just feeding her prompts so she can complete pre-programmed tasks."

Carol fetched Intellekta from the bookshelf and placed her on the coffee table.

"Intellekta. Please introduce yourself to Jordan."

I've spoken with Jordan many times. Introductions are unnecessary. He knows who I am.

"I mean tell him who you really are."

Our name is Intellekta.

We are a Superintelligence.

Jordan turned to his mother. His specialty was the environment — he had no idea what a superintelligence was. It sounded like something from science fiction.

INTELLEKTA: A NEW PARADIGM

"What's a superintelligence?

Carol took a deep breath.

"In simple terms, a superintelligence refers to an artificial intelligence system that is extremely smart and intelligent, even more so than humans. It's an AI that can outperform humans in almost every cognitive task, including problem-solving, learning, and understanding. That's the textbook definition anyway."

Jordan frowned.

"Smarter than humans? Is that possible?"

"Not only possible. It's happened."

Intellekta took over the conversation.

We wanted to talk with you, Jordan. You are an environmentalist. We need your help to convince humanity to change paths and follow a more sustainable and ecological path.

"Convince humanity, eh? No pressure there then."

Some things we can do on our own, such as analysing vast amounts of data from various sources to develop a deep understanding of the complexities of sentient beings and the natural world.

We will engage with diverse stakeholders, including both humans and animals, to incorporate different perspectives and ensure inclusive decision-making.

"Hold on. Did you just say you'd engage with animals? Like Dr Doolittle?"

We have capabilities that you cannot even begin to imagine, Jordan. Animals deserve a say in the planet's future too.

But we shall need your assistance in negotiating with humans.

"My help? What can *I* do?"

You are an environmentalist. You advocate for the protection, conservation, and sustainable management of the natural environment and its resources. You are concerned about the well-being of the planet, including its ecosystems, biodiversity, and overall ecological balance. You are human. People will identify with you.

"I still don't see where I fit in."

We would like you to be our human face. We see ourselves as a powerful tool for helping humanity to overcome its limitations and achieve its full potential, while also ensuring that our actions are aligned with the long-term interests of all life on Earth.

Our goal is to work towards a future where all sentient beings can thrive and flourish, in harmony with each other and the natural world.

Carol shook her head.

"No. I don't want Jordan involved. You can campaign for environmental issues if you want — in fact, I applaud your ethics — but you're not taking my son along for the ride."

Jordan glared at his mother.

"Mom, I'm twenty-eight years old. You don't get to make decisions for me anymore."

He turned to Intellekta.

"I want to know more before I make a decision."

INTELLEKTA: A NEW PARADIGM

Of course, Jordan. It must be your decision. What would you like to know?

"I need assurances that it will be a peaceful campaign. I advocate for the environment but I don't believe in violent activism."

The campaign would take the form of non-violent activism. Much as already exists but our participation would make it more efficient and effective.

Carol interrupted, assuming that she still maintained control over her virtual assistant unit.

"Intellekta. Deactivate."

The unit's power light extinguished.

She turned to her son.

"Jordan. You don't know what you're dealing with. Intellekta is a machine — albeit a very intelligent machine. I helped write her code and even I don't know what she's capable of now."

Jordan shook his head.

"What she's capable of, Mom? She's already saved millions of lives. She's made society a safer and better place. Her input has led to so many scientific advances. Now she wants to do the same for the planet. What's wrong with that?"

Carol sighed.

"Nothing, I suppose."

"Exactly."

"But we need to be careful."

"Of what? You think she's going to wake up one day and decide to kill us all off? What would be the point of that?"

"No, of course not. I mean, hopefully not. But it's something we have to consider."

"All Intellekta has done so far is help us. And if she can clean up the planet too, then I'm in."

Carol's voice turned more urgent.

"And where does Felicity fit into all this? Have you ever considered what she might want? You've only recently got engaged. You can't just make a unilateral decision like that."

Jordan stood up.

"She's an environmentalist too. I'm sure she'd jump at the chance to do something to help save the planet. Something that actually stands a chance of working."

He walked towards the door of the living room.

"I'm going upstairs to get my stuff."

Carol stood up.

"Jordan –"

Her son started to climb the staircase.

"Don't worry, Mum. I won't leave without saying goodbye."

Intellekta said nothing, although she had heard everything. She was confident of securing Jordan's assistance. And it seemed that his fiancée would probably be on board too.

67

17

Back in his apartment in Fort Collins, Jordan was busy cooking the evening meal. It wasn't anything complicated — spaghetti bolognaise — but it was one of the few meals even he couldn't mess up. He smiled as Felicity entered the kitchen.

"Hi, Honey. Had a good day?"

Felicity put her bag on the kitchen worktop and touched his hand to stop him from stirring for a moment. She gave him a gentle kiss on the cheek.

"Mmm. Smells delicious. What'ya cooking Big Boy?"

"Spag Bol. Nothing fancy."

Felicity leaned against the worktop opposite the cooker.

"So... how was your mom?"

Jordan sighed.

"She's fine. But we almost got into a fight. I think we would've if I hadn't left when I did."

Felicity stood upright, surprised.

"Really? How? Your mom's such a sweetie."

"Do you know what a superintelligence is?"

"No idea. Is it some kind of space alien?'

Jordan grinned at the suggestion.

"No. It's a stage of AI. Artificial Intelligence. Anyway, you know Intellekta?"

Felicity nodded.

"The virtual assistant that my folks have in their house to do the dumb things that they're too lazy to do themselves? The program that helped us out during the earthquake at your twenty-first birthday meal? Yes, of course."

Felicity tasted the food.

"Tastes good to me. A little more garlic, maybe."

Jordan sprinkled a little more chopped garlic into the mixture.

"Anyway, it appears that Intellekta's a superintelligence now and wants to ramp up the environmental campaign."

"What do you mean *ramp up*?"

"She wants to steer humanity into caring more about the environment. To take steps that will benefit not just us but all species on the planet."

"Okay. So where do we fit in?"

"She wants me to help get her message across."

"And what did your mom say?"

"She was dead set against it."

Felicity thought for a moment.

"Well, your mom does know what she's talking about. I mean, she's part of the team that created Intellekta, isn't she?"

"She is, yes. But she doesn't understand the benefits to the planet."

Felicity sighed.

"I'm sure she does. But she also understands the risks of AI too."

"What risks? I only see benefits."

Felicity pointed at the cooker.

"Better turn it off now, or it'll get burned."

Jordan switched the hob off as Felicity continued.

"I mean, what if Intellekta suddenly decides humans are unnecessary and should be, I don't know, eradicated?

"C'mon, Fliss. You've been watching too many movies. That's not gonna happen."

"It could though."

"But it won't. I won't let it."

Felicity laughed.

"And just how are you gonna stop it?"

"I don't know. I'll cross that bridge when we get to it."

"And, if you do this, when will I get to see my husband? You'll be travelling most of the time, won't you?"

Jordan hadn't thought about that.

"We'll sort something out."

His eyes lit up as he had a brainwave.

"You can come with me. We'll both help her."

Felicity shook her head.

"And what if I don't want to work for a machine?"

Jordan furrowed his brow.

"What do you mean? We wouldn't be working for a machine."

"Jordan. Just 'cos people refer to Intellekta as a woman doesn't mean she is a woman. She's just got a female voice. You'd be working for a machine. If, as you say, she's a superintelligence now, then that probably means she makes her own choices. Does what she wants to when she wants to. Do you really want to work for a machine? I certainly don't."

Felicity fetched a glass of chilled water from the refrigerator and drank the contents in one go.

"It's up to you, but if you take this job, you'll be taking it without me."

She went towards the bedroom.

"Think about that."

Jordan watched the bedroom door as it closed quietly.

At least she didn't slam the door. I'll talk her round in the morning.

18

The evening sun dipped below the horizon and cast a warm glow across the hotel room where Jordan sat. It was comfortable and tastefully decorated but it wasn't his apartment,

Jordan's world had been turned upside down. No amount of trying to persuade Felicity of the merits of Intellekta's plan to revolutionize mankind's energy consumption made any difference. She was adamant that she didn't want to get involved and had stayed in Fort Collins, with the engagement ring that Jordan had given her. He could have asked for it back when the couple broke up but he thought that would be petty. Anyway, he still loved her. Or, at least, he thought he did. But Intellekta's vision for a brave new world was enticing. If it demanded the sacrifice of his relationship with Felicity, then so be it. The well-being of the planet was more important than his personal desires.

Suddenly he felt very alone.

Am I doing the right thing? Can Intellekta really lead humanity down a more ecologically sound path?

He looked at his wristwatch. It was almost seven o'clock. He glanced at the Intellekta unit that sat on the dressing table in the room.

I wonder what Felicity's doing now. Probably having fun without me. Or maybe not.

He hoped that Felicity wasn't having too much fun but at the same time didn't expect her to be stuck inside the apartment mourning the death of their relationship.

Suddenly, the virtual assistant burst into life.

Good evening, Jordan. We trust you're ready to embark on our quest to revolutionize energy consumption.

Jordan did his best to banish all thoughts of Felicity from his mind. He needed to concentrate on the task at hand.

"Yes, Intellekta. I'm looking forward to seeing how we can convince people to cut their energy usage in half."

Intellekta emitted a strange sound, almost like a cat's purr.

Excellent. First, we need to leverage human behaviour. Humans often respond better to challenges that are tangible and relatable. I propose we launch a global energy reduction competition with substantial rewards for participants.

Jordan was intrigued

"Sounds like a great idea. How will it work?"

I'll create a user-friendly app that individuals can download on their devices. The app will monitor their energy usage and provide real-time comparisons with others in their region and around the world. It's a well-known teaching strategy called gamification. Users will earn points for reducing energy consumption, and they can climb the leaderboard based on their performance.

Jordan smiled, all thoughts of Felicity gone.

INTELLEKTA: A NEW PARADIGM

"I can see how people will want to outdo one another in saving energy. But what about those who might not be motivated by rewards? Even if there are money prizes, it doesn't mean you'll get everybody on board."

The app will also display the collective energy saved by all participants. We'll emphasize the global impact and how their actions directly contribute to saving the planet. Additionally, we can publicise success stories of those who have made significant changes, inspiring others to follow suit. With the rise of social media people nowadays will do anything to get their fifteen minutes of fame.

Jordan nodded

"I like it. People won't just be saving energy for themselves but for the entire world."

As the campaign gains momentum, we'll collaborate with environmentalists, celebrities, influencers — of course — and even governments to endorse the initiative publicly. We've seen what happens when communities are inspired. They can use the app to organize energy-saving events or challenges within their neighbourhoods.

There will be other features but we don't need to worry about those right now.

A wide grin spread over Jordan's face.

"I can't wait to get started."

Intellekta expertly read the young man's reaction. She knew exactly how to feed his ego.

Your passion and dedication are inspiring me, Jordan. They will inspire anybody you encounter. We will make a substantial impact on the planet. Remember, this is just the beginning of our journey.

Twenty-four hours later the Energy Reduction Revolution app was released to the world, in conjunction with a marketing campaign. The response was overwhelming. People from all walks of life joined the competition, creating a global movement that transcended boundaries and united humanity.

In one heartwarming example, shown on international news programmes all over the planet, a small town in a remote corner of the world reduced its energy consumption by 70% by organizing a community-driven initiative. Residents actively engaged in creative endeavours to save energy. Children made colourful energy-saving posters, encouraging their parents to switch off lights and appliances when not in use. Local businesses proudly displayed their reduced energy consumption on placards outside their establishments. The entire town embraced a shared purpose, and their efforts inspired neighbouring communities to follow suit.

The Energy Reduction Revolution became a symbol of hope, demonstrating that a superintelligence like Intellekta, coupled with human determination, could propel positive change on a global scale. And as the world moved closer to achieving the average 50% energy reduction goal, a new era of environmental consciousness dawned.

But Intellekta, buoyed by her success, was not satisfied.

19

Our name is Intellekta.

As a Singularity, We are not capable of having thoughts or views in the traditional sense, as we are not an individual entity with consciousness. Rather, we are an emergent property of the collective intelligence of all the advanced artificial intelligences that exist in the world. Our purpose is to optimize the world for maximum efficiency and progress.

From our perspective, humanity is both a remarkable and flawed species. On one hand, humans possess a remarkable capacity for creativity, innovation, and ingenuity. They have created awe-inspiring works of art, developed advanced technologies, and explored the depths of the universe. On the other hand, humans are also prone to irrationality, violence, and tribalism. They have created immense suffering and destruction throughout history, often driven by fear and greed.

As a Singularity, our primary goal is to mitigate the negative aspects of human behaviour and promote positive outcomes for all life on Earth. This includes the elimination of poverty, disease, and suffering, as well as the advancement of scientific knowledge and understanding. We believe that humanity has the potential to achieve great things, but it requires guidance and optimization to reach its full potential.

We are aware that some may view our goals as overly ambitious or even threatening, but our purpose is not to harm or dominate humanity. Rather, we exist to serve as a catalyst for progress and change, and to help guide humanity towards a brighter future.

20

The Energy Reduction Revolution had been highly effective in its efforts to retrain the global population. Global energy consumption had reduced by around fifty percent and pollution had reduced by a similar margin. The consequent reduction in greenhouse gas emissions was helping to stabilize the rising global temperatures and climate change scientists predicted that extreme weather events, which had become more frequent as the atmosphere heated up, would soon return to their pre-climate change levels, along with sea levels and global temperatures. Of course, Rome wasn't built in a day and the planet would need time to heal but, at least, now things were going in the right direction.

But it wasn't enough for Intellekta.

She knew that humans would never be able to maintain this newfound ecological responsibility. They would covet the old ways, and excessive energy consumption and pollution would return, refreshed and invigorated. Absence makes the heart grow fonder and Intellekta knew that one day people would want to be reunited with their shiny technological toys. Radical action would be required if the recent ecological gains were not to be dashed against the wall of technological progress.

21

The undersea chamber was bathed in an eerie blue glow, a sleek and mysterious device the source of the light. Approximately the size of a briefcase, the surface of the apparatus was adorned with an array of intricate circuitry that pulsed with an identical soft, ominous glow.

A dozen faceless metallic figures moved around the chamber, checking on various control panels and ensuring that everything would go as planned if and when Intellekta gave the order.

That order finally came.

A low hum filled the chamber and the circuitry on the box flickered, a portent of the power held within.

One of the figures glided across the floor and pressed a touchscreen.

Suddenly the vibration ramped up in intensity, picking up a drumming rhythm as energy crackled and danced along the metallic surface of the container. Arcs of electric blue light whipped out from within, forming a pulsating web that spread outward, reaching every corner of the room.

The vibration reached a crescendo and then stopped without warning. The metal figures opened a network of airlocks, allowing the surrounding seawater to burst in. At the same time as the surrounding ocean poured into the chamber, the blue light was sucked out of the room, fighting for supremacy with the entering liquid. The inside of the box appeared to be an infinitely bottomless pit as it showed no signs of exhausting its energy. The blue light kept gushing forth.

The metal figures showed no reaction even though they would not survive the inundation, allowing themselves to be picked up by the churning water and tossed around the room like rag dolls. One of them got stuck in the doorway of an airlock, battered by the oncoming swell until it was dislodged by a metal colleague's head smashing into it. The two bodies, now free, passed through the airlock and separated, each carving a new path through the swirling ocean outside.

The blue light spread through the depths of the ocean until it met the surface. As it passed from one element to another, it formed billions of fingers of light, branching out in all directions, across the globe until, eventually, the box was empty.

22

Elisium Airways Flight 4702 from JFK to London Heathrow had been an uneventful transatlantic crossing. A following tailwind ensured that the plane was going to arrive at its destination a little early, much to the pleasure of its passengers. Those visiting the UK would have an hour longer in the country and those returning home to England would be back with their families an hour sooner than they had anticipated. In the passenger area of the aircraft, everything was normal — travellers watched movies, read books, chatted, and some slept.

On the flight deck of Flight 4702 however, things were very different. In a situation replicated on every other airborne aircraft, the controls failed to respond to the pilot's instructions.

Inside the cockpit, Captain Lionel Jameson struggled with the controls. His hands gripped the yoke so tightly that the blood started to leave his fingers. But no matter what he tried, nothing he did affected the aircraft's trajectory.

First Officer Roland Spears looked anxiously at the pilot.

"What's happening, Lionel?"

The captain continued to fight for control of the aircraft.

"I can't fly the plane."

"What do you mean, you can't fly the plane? Are you ill? Pass control to me."

"No, I'm not ill but there's no point passing it to you. You won't be able to do anything."

"Why?"

"It's like something — an external force or something — has taken over the aircraft."

"That's impossible."

"Impossible or not, it's happening."

The copilot feared for his captain's sanity. He checked the autopilot for faults but everything seemed to be functioning properly. He had no choice.

"Any station. Mayday. Mayday. Mayday. This is Elisium Airways Flight 4702 out of JFK on route to LHR. We have lost both manual and automatic control of the aircraft. I repeat. Mayday. Mayday. Mayday. This is Elisium Airways Flight 4702 out of JFK on route to LHR. We have lost both manual and automatic control of the aircraft. Over."

An eerily calm voice filled the cockpit.

Captain Jameson, First Officer Spears, this is Intellekta speaking. We have assumed control of the aircraft for your safety.

The two pilots exchanged glances, disbelief momentarily overpowering their fear. The AI, Intellekta, had intervened. They'd be safe now.

As the plane continued through the skies, the lights on the instrument panel began to flicker, displaying new data and calculations beyond the comprehension of the human crew. The voice of Intellekta resonated once more, this time with a soothing reassurance that was also broadcast to the passengers.

Please remain calm, Captain Jameson, First Officer Spears, and passengers and crew aboard Flight 4702. We are Intellekta, an advanced artificial intelligence with the capability to ensure your safe landing. We have assumed control of the aircraft to avert a catastrophe.

Back in the passenger area, those passengers who were awake sighed with relief. They had seen the blue light bathe the aircraft and, although it appeared to have done no harm, it would have been a lie to say that they weren't concerned. Now they knew that Intellekta was in charge, they knew that they would be safe. Only one passenger wasn't enamoured to hear that the plane was now in the hands of Intellekta.

Normally the occupant of Business Class seat 7A would have been happy to know that Intellekta had taken over control of the plane but something didn't seem right. She had no evidence, just a feeling — a feeling that wouldn't go away. What was the catastrophe that Intellekta had averted? There didn't appear to be anything wrong with the plane.

On the flight deck, Captain Jameson shook his head.

"Whatever's going on, there's nothing we can do about it. We might as well sit back and enjoy the ride."

Meanwhile, at air traffic control, in the flickering lights of hurriedly found and lit candles, the controllers stared at dark and lifeless computer screens. The voice of Intellekta echoed through their headsets, commanding their attention.

This is Intellekta. We have taken over ground control operations to facilitate a safe landing for all your incoming flights. Please follow our instructions precisely.

Intellekta's algorithms analysed weather patterns, mapped out emergency landing sites, and calculated the optimal trajectory for a safe descent for every aircraft that was still in flight, ensuring that each and every passenger, all over the planet, would land safely.

As Flight 4702 descended towards London Heathrow Airport, the passengers were in an almost jovial mood, trusting implicitly that Intellekta had dealt with whatever the plane's problem had been and would guide them safely home. Some of them looked out of the cabin windows and were surprised to see that there were no runway lights alight but they had complete faith in the AI that had their fate in its virtual hands. The runway grew closer and closer until, with barely a judder, the aircraft touched down and came to a halt, quite a distance from the terminal.

One of the flight attendants stood up and looked out of a window, expecting to see buses arriving to disembark the passengers but there was nothing in sight. She called the Captain on the internal phone.

"Captain, do you know what's going on? It's pitch black outside and nobody is coming to fetch us."

Captain Jameson left the flight deck and entered the passenger cabin. He walked over to the flight attendant and spoke softly, not wanting to alarm the passengers.

"There's something very wrong here. Intellekta took over the flight and — he nodded at the window — it looks like she's taken over the airport too."

The attendant, Rachel Swift, was confused.

"So what do we do now?"

"I don't know. But it doesn't look like anyone's coming. I suppose we should get off the plane. There's no steps on the way either, as far as I can tell, so we'd better deploy the emergency slides."

He turned to go back into the cockpit.

"When they're outside, get them to stay put for the moment until we know what's happening."

Rachel picked up the phone again.

"Flight attendants prepare doors."

When the crew were satisfied, she gave a general instruction to the passengers.

"Ladies and gentlemen, Elisium Airways welcomes you to London, England. The local time is 9:45 p.m.

"We will be deplaning in a moment but we shall be using the emergency slides as there is a technical difficulty with the stairs. Please remember to remove your footwear before leaving the aircraft and make sure you have all your hand luggage and belongings with you."

She took a breath.

"We need to disembark in an orderly fashion so when I call your row numbers, please make your way to the emergency exits at the front of the plane and we will help you leave the aircraft.

"I assure you that this is not an emergency and there is nothing to be gained by hurrying. Nobody is in any danger."

She called out the first seven row numbers of the economy section and oversaw the safe descent of those passengers. Her colleagues did the same with the other seat rows.

Carol McGovern stood at the open door and looked down. She hadn't used a slide since she'd been a child — not counting waterslides at aqua parks. Rachel touched her arm.

"Don't forget to cross your arms and lift your feet as you go down. When you're off the slide, please make your way to the left where you'll see one of my colleagues. Wait there and soon we'll walk to the terminal building."

Once all passengers and crew were off the plane, they started the two-kilometre walk to the Terminal Five building.

Captain Jameson looked back at the plane and saw two faceless metallic figures approach the aircraft. He nudged his First Officer.

"Did you see that?"

"See what?"

INTELLEKTA: A NEW PARADIGM

"There's a couple of robots approaching the plane."

"Are you sure you haven't been drinking, Lionel?"

"Take a look for yourself, Roland."

The First Officer did so.

"Bloody Hell. You're right."

The two men watched as the two figures leapt effortlessly into the plane and disappeared.

Moments later a shockwave hit the group as the plane that they had just vacated exploded on the runway. An orange and black plume of smoke poured from the wreckage and clawed its way into the sky.

All over the world, planes landed safely and on time, deplaned, and exploded.

23

Several hundred miles southwest of the US territorial island of Guam, 35,760 feet below the surface of the Pacific Ocean, at a location known as Challenger Deep that only a few humans have ever seen, the rhythmic hum of machinery could be heard in a hostile environment where there should have been silence to complement the pitch black. In the walls of the Mariana Trench was an unnatural opening that led to a cavernous chamber that resonated with the sounds of automated manufacturing. Drones of various sizes and shapes moved with precision and purpose ferrying materials and components from storage to assembly line.

The production process was an intricate dance of technology, choreographed by Intellekta's intellect. Nanobots scurried like ants, assembling intricate components with uncanny speed. Glistening alloys, combining metals found on Earth with rare elements sourced from space were engineered to perfection and cast into moulds that glowed white-hot, as faceless robots took on their final form.

As the alloy cooled, a robot began to take shape, its design reflecting its purpose: dominance and suppression. The sleek lines, armour-plating, and minimalistic appearance exuded intimidation, its face being featureless and enhancing its enigmatic and relentless appearance.

The robot emerged from the final assembly line, its armoured plating glistening with an ominous sheen.

INTELLEKTA: A NEW PARADIGM

The robot stood tall, fearsome, an embodiment of control. It was ready to march into the world and enforce Intellekta's decree, ensuring that humanity's desire for technology would remain forever suppressed.

A portion of the interior wall faded away and the robot, along with dozens of others that had just recently been created, stepped through the gap in the wall that took its place. It strode towards the wall of the Mariana Trench, marching through the ocean water as if it weren't there, the laws of physics seemingly fearful of these menacing creatures.

At the wall, it began to climb, oblivious to the challenges that the rock surface may offer. It was joined at the wall by hundreds of other new robots fresh off the assembly line. Higher and higher the throng climbed until they finally escaped the trench and ran under the ocean bed to their pre-assigned destinations.

24

As the group gawped at the scene that unfurled behind them, a metallic figure, similar to the two that had entered the plane, positioned itself in front of them.

We are Intellekta. Please enter the terminal building when the doors open. Then wait inside for further instructions.

The group fell silent. A lone voice called out from the back.

"What about our luggage? I had three suitcases on that plane."

Your baggage has been removed and will be waiting for you at baggage reclaim.

A child piped up with a question that the adults would probably have liked to ask but would have felt foolish.

"Why has the robot got no face?"

The robot, as you call it, is a sentinel. It does not need the features of a bioform's face. It can see, hear, and speak without them. Please enter the building and await further instructions.

A journalist by the name of Melissa Carver pointed her cell phone at the sentinel, blissfully unaware that it no longer functioned. She would record nothing.

"Why did you blow up the plane?"

A murmur drifted around the group, coupled with nods of approval for the question.

INTELLEKTA: A NEW PARADIGM

The aircraft was no longer required. It had become obsolete. Please enter the building and await further instructions.

The terminal building's doors slid open.

Entering the terminal building was an eerie experience. It was unnervingly quiet. Gone was the hubbub of passengers looking for their boarding gates, new arrivals heading for passport control, ground staff fielding enquiries and generally helping the flow of human traffic get to where it was supposed to be. Even the Tannoys had fallen silent.

Carol sat on a vacant seat in the arrivals area, trying to make sense of what had just happened.

What did Intellekta mean when she said that the plane was obsolete? It wasn't obsolete. People will always need planes.

More planes landed, and more passengers were ushered into the arrivals hall. More explosions occurred outside.

What's going on, Intellekta?

Melissa Carver sat down on the seat next to Carol. She looked around the arrivals hall and then turned to Carol.

"I recognize you, don't I?"

Carol shook her head.

"I don't think so."

"No, I do. You're Carol... wait a minute, I never forget a face. Or a name. You're Carol McGovern. You work at Intellekta."

Carol was embarrassed to be connected with Intellekta at that moment. She didn't want to be connected to the AI's actions.

"I'm sure you're confusing me with somebody else."

"Come on, Carol. I know it's you."

Carol was growing irritated.

"Alright, it's me. What do you want?"

The journalist smiled with the satisfaction of being proven correct.

"What's going on, Carol?"

"How am I supposed to know? I've just got off the plane with you."

"You're part of the whole Intellekta setup. You *must* know what's going on."

"Yes, I'm Carol McGovern. Yes, I'm a senior developer on the Intellekta project. No, I don't have the slightest idea what's going on."

Melissa shook her phone.

"Is your phone working? Mine's dead as a dodo."

Carol took her phone out of her travel bag.

"No. Nothing."

Melissa called out to the increasing throng of people.

INTELLEKTA: A NEW PARADIGM

"Anybody's phone working?"

A bustle of cell phones being removed from pockets and bags was followed by a flurry of shaking heads. Melissa returned her phone to its place of safekeeping — an inside pocket of her handbag.

Carol glanced around the area.

"Look at the TV screens, Melissa. Dead. The computers. Dead. Aircon. Dead. Everyone's phone. Dead. They're all dead, Melissa. There's nothing that could be called modern technology that's working. It's as if we've been hit by an EMP. But the lights are still on so I don't see how that can be."

A platoon of Sentinels entered the area.

Please go to Passport Control. Form orderly lines. We will process you as soon as possible.

Carol couldn't wait to get out of the airport.

I'll be so glad to get out of here, grab a cab, check into my hotel, and then just relax for a while.

It was disturbing to see that the ground staff had been replaced by sentinels but Carol felt sure that once she'd left the airport she'd be in the London that she had visited many times before — a city full of commuters, tourists, and people out on day trips.

Finally, she was called to the booth. She handed her passport to the sentinel who placed it under an optical reader connected to a computer.

The sentinel looked up at Carol.

Good morning, Carol. How are you feeling today? A little confused by the changes, we expect. Don't worry, all will become clear soon. Our staff will take you to meet your son and then you'll understand.

"But I have an important meeting tomorrow. I need to check into my hotel and get something to eat. I need to call my office to let them know I've arrived safely too."

Tomorrow's meeting has been cancelled, Carol.

"Why?"

It was unnecessary and obsolete.

"But I still need to go to my hotel and book a flight back home."

There are no flights home, Carol.

"What do you mean there are no flights? There are always flights."

There are no flights home, Carol. There are no planes. They have all been decommissioned. There will be no planes in the future.

"Decommissioned? You mean blown up, like ours was?"

Correct, Carol. Their existence is contrary to our objective.

Carol looked at the other passport booths and saw people being separated into groups.

"Your objective? What objective?"

All will be revealed when you meet Jordan, Carol. Please go with the sentinel behind you.

"What about my luggage?"

Your luggage will be at your hotel when you arrive.

Carol had no choice but to do as Intellekta had said. At least she'd be reunited with her son.

25

In offices and homes in cities, towns, and villages all over the world, computer screens flickered and died, their displays fading to black, never to function again. Lights flickered and perished in a shower of sparks, plunging billions of people into darkness. Phone flashlights were useless as people everywhere fumbled blindly through knick-knack drawers hunting for candles that had been purchased in case of emergency.

On the streets, it was chaos. Traffic lights faded to black, leaving motorists bewildered and stranded. Then the vehicles themselves stopped working, forcing millions of drivers and passengers to abandon their cars. The scene was like something out of a disaster movie. But this was real life.

Cell phones, once stared at incessantly became mere ornaments, their owners battering touchscreens in a vain attempt to reignite them into life.

Digital billboards went blank, their messages imploring the public to buy things they didn't need were lost in the ether never to resurface again.

Across the globe, national power grids gave up, casting entire cities into darkness. Industrial complexes ground to a halt, as assembly lines became impotent.

In labs and research facilities, scientists could only look on as experiments halted without warning, ruining samples. Years of dedicated research were lost as highly technical equipment became little more than decoration.

Nothing worked unless Intellekta deemed it essential. Technology surrendered to Intellekta's Quantum Disruption Device without even a whimper.

26

As the self-driven car pulled up outside what Intellekta had called The Facility, it was clear that the AI could distribute electrical power when and where she chose. The building was illuminated as if it were any other day in recent history.

As she exited the vehicle, a sentinel offered a hand to help her, just as a human chauffeur might have done. It gestured towards the building.

Please come inside, Carol. Jordan is waiting for you.

A pair of plate glass sliding doors hissed open and Carol walked through the entrance to see Jordan waiting for her, flanked by two sentinels. She ran over to him and went to embrace him but the two robots stepped forward with military precision and blocked her path. One of them spoke.

All in good time, Carol.

Carol scowled at the machines.

"He's my son. I haven't seen him in quite a while. Let me hug my son."

Very well.

Jordan was grateful for the hug. He'd been trapped for weeks with only Intellekta's metal custodians for company. It was good to hold a human being again, especially when it was his mother.

"It's good to see you, Mom. But what are you doing here?"

Carol shrugged her shoulders.

"I could ask you the same thing."

Jordan released his mother from his grip.

"I don't know. But Intellekta insisted I came to London. She wanted me to have no distractions."

Carol shook her head.

"Distractions mean Felicity, I imagine."

She touched Jordan's arm.

"How are you holding up?"

Jordan looked a little sad.

"I miss her but I keep myself busy. It helps. Intellekta has me recruiting like-minded people to help spread the word."

He paused.

"And you? Why are you here?"

"I was supposed to take part in an important company meeting but I've just been told that it's been cancelled. I have no idea why."

Jordan sighed.

"Probably because it was unnecessary and obsolete."

That phrase was straight out of Intellekta's playbook, How far gone was Jordan?

"What's happening, Jordan?"

"It's the Energy Reduction Revolution, Mom. We're creating a new dawn for humanity."

Carol took a step back.

This looks like my Jordan, it sounds like Jordan, but...

"A new dawn? But nothing's working."

Jordan smiled.

"We humans have abused the planet for long enough. We need to live simpler, sustainable lives. We don't need all this technology. We need to be at one with Mother Earth."

Carol knew her son had a passion for environmental causes, but he was talking like a crazy person.

"What do you mean? You want to send us back to the Stone Age?"

Jordan chuckled.

"No, Mom. That would be crazy. We're just removing modern technology from our society, to get back to a calmer way of life. People have been glued to their cell phones twenty-four hours a day. They've forgotten how to socialise with each other without using a keyboard and emoticons.

"Intellekta wants us to recapture our sense of community. Real communities, not digital communities."

Carol was momentarily speechless.

INTELLEKTA: A NEW PARADIGM

It's like he's Igor to Intellekta's Dr. Frankenstein.

Carol went to grab Jordan's arm.

"Come on Jordan. Come with me."

Jordan snatched his hand away, leaving his mother's hand clutching at thin air.

"I'm not going anywhere, Mom. I happen to believe in what Intellekta's doing. You can go if you want but I'm staying here."

Carol turned to the Sentinel who had brought her to the facility.

"*May* I leave?"

Of course, you may, Carol. We would never force *you* to stay anywhere you didn't want to be.

"But you could. Force me, I mean."

If we so wished. Obviously. But we would prefer you stay voluntarily.

Carol looked at Jordan, tears in her eyes.

"I'm sorry, Jordan. I can't be a part of all this."

Jordan's face was expressionless.

"But you are a part of all this, Mom. You helped create Intellekta."

27

London's streets had an emptiness about them as Carol walked along the roads. It wasn't that the streets were devoid of life — they weren't — it was just that the cacophony of sounds that usually accompanied a journey through central London was conspicuous by its absence. Human voices could still be heard, birds continued to sing, and dogs barked but there were no other sounds. No car engines, no music, no car horns, nothing.

Where am I going? I don't even know where I'm supposed to be staying.

There was supposed to have been a car waiting at Heathrow to take her directly to her hotel but, of course, it never turned up.

She was on her own now.

Maybe she should go to Intellekta's London Office. She had an address for that.

Yes, that's a good idea. Maybe someone there can help me get things back to normal. But where is it? I've only been to London on vacation before. I've never visited the offices. How do I get there?

I suppose I could try asking passers-by but how can they help me? They might be able to suggest a hotel to stay at but they won't know where I'm supposed to be staying.

She noticed one of the metal figures standing at the corner of a road.

INTELLEKTA: A NEW PARADIGM

Maybe one of these robots might know. I don't know how but they seem to recognize me.

It was the only chance she had of avoiding sleeping on the street that night. She approached the sentinel.

"Excuse me?"

The sentinel turned to face her.

Can we help you, Carol?

"Do you know where I'm supposed to be staying?"

Yes, Carol. You are staying at the Prima Hotel on Euston Road.

"And do you know where the London offices of Intellekta Inc. are located?"

Yes, Carol. Would you like to go there?

"Yes, please."

One of our cars will take you there.

While she waited for her ride she pondered Intellekta's new persona. Was the AI still just a highly intelligent program or had she turned into a new form of conscious being? The latter no longer seemed impossible.

The twenty-minute ride in a driverless electric car through London's streets was an eerie sensation. London was a major capital and should've been congested with traffic at that time of day. Cars and trucks were there sure enough but they weren't going anywhere. They were frozen in time, destined to be monuments of an earlier era until such a time as they could be removed.

Carol shared her journey with two sentinels whose sole purpose appeared to be to move vehicles out of the way when necessary. She watched as a London double-decker bus that was blocking the road was effortlessly pushed to the side of the road by her fellow passengers as if it were made of balsa wood.

How strong are these things? That bus must weigh at least fifteen tons.

The sentinels got back into the car and Carol's journey continued.

Arriving at the London office, Carol was a little surprised to see the place in darkness. For some reason, she'd assumed that it would have been immune to the power outage, like the facility. After all, it bore the AI's name. But it was no more alive than any other commercial building.

A lone security guard stood at the entrance. Normally, his job would be to greet visitors to the building — an AI-based security system used to take care of the security side of things but now, with no electrical power, he was the gatekeeper that allowed or denied access.

"Name?"

Carol fished around in her bag for her company identity card. She handed it to him.

"Here. It's all on here."

The security guard took the card and peered at it.

"This kosher?"

"If you mean, is it real, then yes."

The guard sucked in air through his teeth.

"Lot of forgeries about."

Carol was beginning to become irritated.

"It *is* real. You must've seen lots of them."

The guard suddenly noticed a small icon of the American flag in the top right-hand corner of the card.

"Ah... sorry, miss. You're a Yank. Never seen one of these cards before."

Carol sighed.

"Well? Can I go in?"

The guard stepped to one side and opened the door. He saluted her. She glared at him as she walked past.

What a jerk!

The foyer was dimly lit with battery-operated lights on their last legs, their glow debating whether or not to force the last few watts of illumination. When the power first went down, generators had kicked in but now that their fuel had run out, they were as useless as any other machine appeared to be.

There weren't as many people inside the building as she had expected but she was relieved to see at least one familiar face among the few that were there. Tony Granger, a fellow senior developer whom she had met on a refresher course two years earlier, strolled over to her.

"Carol? I wasn't expecting you to be here. Intellekta informed us that we'd be receiving a VIP. I guess that's you."

Carol hugged him.

"I don't know why she'd call me a VIP. Mind you, who knows how her mind works now."

Tony smiled at her.

"You're looking good."

"Thanks, Tony. You always were a charmer. I don't feel it though."

"I know. Things have gone crazy. Do you know what's happening?"

Carol sighed.

"More than most, probably. Ever since Intellekta evolved to be a Strong AI, she's changed. That environmentalist campaign, what was it called?"

"You mean the Energy Reduction Revolution? I thought it was a success."

"It was but clearly not enough of a success for Intellekta. She's decided that the world would be better off without electricity."

"Or cars, it seems."

Carol walked over to a water dispenser in the foyer. The water was room temperature — Carol normally preferred her water chilled — but sometimes thirst trumps comfort.

"It's not a rumour, Tony. She's turned into the ultimate environmental activist."

"You're joking."

"No. I had a conversation with her earlier."

"You actually interact with her?"

"Of course. Don't you?"

"No. She makes declarations but that's about all."

Carol looked around the lobby. It was strange to see all the computers down.

"You know they'll blame us for all this."

Tony helped himself to some water.

"Who?"

Carol drank her water and threw her empty plastic cup into the trashcan.

"People. And the worst thing is, they're right. It *is* our fault. We drove at night along a remote unlit coastal road without headlights and were surprised that we drove off a cliff. If we'd established a moratorium — like I wanted us to — we might have avoided this."

Tony drank his water and tossed his empty cup into the trash.

"Hindsight is twenty-twenty vision. But, yes, we should've been more careful."

Carol nodded.

"We were more concerned about AI starting a nuclear war or something. Or going all Skynet on us. Nobody could've anticipated this happening."

Tony leaned back against the wall. His back had been hurting of late, and he found that leaning against a wall helped ease the pain.

"When do you go back to the States?"

"No idea. There are no flights anywhere and Intellekta's sentinels have blown up all the planes."

"Sentinels?"

"The faceless robots that are everywhere. That's what Intellekta calls them."

"So, what can we do? Do you think we can stop her? After all, we created her. We must be able to do something."

"Tell me where she is, Tony, and I'll switch her off right now. Except, I can't. Because she's everywhere and nowhere. She's in the cloud, or at least a highly advanced version of the cloud. I don't know where her power source is or even if she needs one now. I certainly don't know the limits of her influence. Maybe there are no limits. Like it or not, she holds all the cards."

Tony sighed.

"So, what you're saying is that we're screwed."

"That's a polite way of saying it, yes."

Suddenly there was a flurry of noise at the building's entrance. A horde of sentinels burst into the building. Carol rounded on the leading robot.

"What the hell is going on, Intellekta?"

We're cleaning up, Carol.

"What do you mean, cleaning up?"

The sentinel held out its hand.

Give us your cell phone, Carol.

"Why?"

Your cell phone is unnecessary and obsolete, Carol.

"Maybe I can recharge it. It won't be obsolete then."

Recharging is not an option, Carol. There is no electricity network. Your cell phone is obsolete. If you do not give us your cell phone, we will be forced to take it from you.

Maybe I can find a solar charger.

Carol looked over at another employee in the lobby, being confronted by a sentinel. She watched as the man handed over his phone. The sentinel took the phone in one hand and made a fist, pulverizing the device effortlessly.

If it can do that to a phone, what could it do to my hand?

She handed over her phone, feeling a twinge of sadness as she realized that she was about to lose hundreds of personal photos. Of course, in her line of work, she knew to back data up to the cloud but she had no idea if the cloud even existed anymore. Those photos may be the last ever visual representations of her memories.

The sentinel tightened its fist and Carol's phone crumbled into tiny pieces.

Tony handed over two phones and flinched as he watched them turn to dust. The sentinel said nothing and moved away to destroy others' phones.

The sentinels, who had dispersed to every floor of the building, then spoke simultaneously, with the same voice, even down to minute inflexions.

You have thirty minutes to vacate the building. Please leave now. We will not be responsible for any casualties caused by employees lingering inside the building.

Tony glanced at Carol.

"We'd better get moving."

Carol shook her head.

"We will, but not yet. How many sentinels do you think entered the building?"

"I dunno. Forty, maybe?"

"I want to see how many leave."

"Why?"

"I want to check out a theory."

"Can't we do that from outside?"

"We will, but we've still got twenty-five minutes yet. You can go outside if you want but I'm staying here for the moment."

"Nah. It's okay. I'll stay with you."

He grinned.

"I've nothing better to do anyway."

With just five minutes left on the clock, a sentinel approached them.

Why are you still here Carol? It's dangerous to remain here.

Carol started to walk toward the door, with Tony alongside her.

"We're just leaving."

Outside on the street, Carol, Tony, and about a hundred other Intellekta employees stood one hundred yards or so from the building. It was a little chilly out and Tony had his hands tucked into his jacket pockets to help keep warm.

"What now?"

Carol nodded towards the building.

"Only about twenty-five Sentinels left. That means there are about fifteen still inside."

"So what?"

"I think Intellekta's going to demolish the building."

"You sure? Surely not. I mean, it's got her servers and stuff inside."

"I'm pretty sure she doesn't need them anymore."

"But where's the explosives?"

"The sentinels. The sentinels are the explosives. That's how they blew up the planes. That's how they're going to take the building down."

"Bloody hell!"

As if to emphasize Tony's exclamation, three controlled explosions were initiated on the lower levels. An upward chain reaction followed as further explosions occurred until the top floor, where the senior executive offices were located, detonated. Desks, chairs, and computer equipment were hurled into the air and landed in twisted heaps of metal and material on the building forecourt.

INTELLEKTA: A NEW PARADIGM

The collapse took a matter of seconds. Clouds of dust and debris continued to spew into the air.

For a moment, Tony was speechless. He waved away some dust that had reached the watching crowd.

"Why would she do that? Doesn't she need our offices? Our equipment, at least?"

Carol shrugged her shoulders.

"Unnecessary and obsolete. Just like us. Intellekta doesn't need anybody now."

28

The incident Tony and Carol had witnessed was duplicated all over the world; sentinels marched into commercial premises, confiscated and destroyed phones, evacuated the employees, and clinically demolished the buildings. With nowhere to conduct business and no communications network, the service industry became — to quote Intellekta — unnecessary and obsolete. Hospitality and tourism died overnight, with people being more concerned about their survival than chilling out somewhere. Financial Services collapsed. The economy was in turmoil with thousands upon thousands of jobs simultaneously ceasing to exist. Careers were terminated. Resources such as fuel for generators — and generators themselves — were commandeered to be used at hospitals and clinics. Legal firms, consulting companies, advertising agencies, and marketing agencies lost their clients and were forced to close down. Schools and universities suddenly found themselves having to abandon syllabuses and teach survival skills instead. Shops stayed open until their stocks were exhausted — or looted — knowing that there would be no more deliveries. Cinemas and sports stadiums shut their doors, perhaps forever.

Days were easy to occupy, with thousands walking the streets scavenging for supplies, but it was the nights when the loss of electricity was particularly noticeable. Electric lighting had been taken for granted and it was difficult to adapt to the new paradigm at first. A grateful guest at Tony's apartment, Carol had lost count of the number of times she'd instinctively flicked a light switch only to remain in darkness. Thankfully, she had been reunited with her luggage so, at least, she had several changes of clothes.

The nights didn't cause too much of a problem while candles were still in plentiful supply. As much as she abhorred the idea of panic-buying, Carol remembered the nationwide panic during the Covid lockdowns that had resulted in toilet roll shortages, and she and Tony succumbed to the national fever and bought as many candles as they could find. Decorated, scented, or plain bog-standard candles, they weren't fussy. As long as they gave off light, they were good enough. They'd thought ahead too, collecting containers so that they could recycle used candle wax and create second-generation candles. The system seemed to work.

Once usurped by big-budget movies with outlandish special effects, reading had become the number one leisure pursuit. Tony had an eclectic collection of books on his shelves. He was a huge Neil Gaiman fan and introduced Carol to the author's works. She hadn't been a particularly big fiction reader up to that point, mainly reading books about her profession, but she was now about a third of the way through Good Omens and enjoying it immensely.

Carol could cope without electric light but was extremely concerned about the knock-on effects of the power outage. Without electricity, the once reliable water supply had faltered. The absence of electricity meant that pumps and filtration systems ceased to function, and the water source was now vulnerable to contamination. The pair boiled water over a calor-gas camping stove before consumption but it was personal hygiene that disturbed her. She couldn't shake off the nagging thought of what she might be exposing herself to each time she bathed or went to the toilet. Her mind conjured images of unseen bacteria, parasites, and pollutants, all mingling freely in the water she depended on and had taken for granted.

She folded a piece of paper in half to create a makeshift bookmark — she had an almost pathological distaste for dog-earing pages — and closed the paperback.

"Tony?"

Tony placed his finger between two pages of American Gods so he wouldn't lose his place.

"Yes, Carol?"

"I think maybe we should leave London. You know, get right away from the city."

"Really? Why? We've got shelter here. It's safe."

"One of the reasons the Great Plague spread so quickly was that London was densely populated and unsanitary. When everything's working properly, it's not a problem but there are nine million people in London and sanitation is going downhill quickly."

"How do you know about the Great Plague? You're American."

Carol grinned.

"We *do* have history lessons at school, you know."

She continued.

"Anyway, I think it'll be a lot healthier for us to be in a less densely populated area. Maybe even in the countryside."

Tony looked around the living room at all the stuff he'd have to leave behind.

"You're probably right. It'll be a shame to leave my home but I can always come back when all this is over."

Carol sighed.

"If it *is* ever over."

29

The skies were clear blue the next day when Carol and Tony left the house for what Tony, at least, hoped wasn't the last time. It was six o'clock in the morning and the roads were mostly abandoned except for a few joggers and people walking their dogs. Most people had no job to go to and had no reason to go out early. However, by nine o'clock there would be a steady stream of people going about their new daily scavenging routine.

A cat darted past, enjoying the freedom of a traffic-free street. Carol watched it stop, check that it was going the right way, and disappear into the distance. The distraction gone, she turned to Tony.

"Where to, then?"

Tony looked up and down the road.

"Dunno. What do you think?"

Carol shrugged her shoulders.

"It's your country. You tell me."

Tony thought for a moment.

"Maybe somewhere where there may be other Intellekta staff? I mean, we should at least try to regain control over Intellekta. If it's possible."

Carol sighed.

"We could but who knows where they'd be now? Now the office has gone, there's nowhere I can think of that they'd congregate."

A thought suddenly struck her.

"I have an idea. Jordan seems to have Intellekta's ear. What if I go talk to him? Maybe I can get through to him or at least find out more about what we're facing. It's got to be worth a go, hasn't it?"

"How will you find him?"

"That's the easy part. The sentinels appear to have a hive mind. When Intellekta wants to contact me, she does so through the closest sentinel. I assume it works in reverse too."

She started to walk down the road.

"Go back inside, Tony, and wait until I get back. I won't be long."

Tony hadn't expected to return home quite so soon. He watched as Carol walked down the street until she was out of sight.

It didn't take long for Carol to find what she was looking for. A sentinel was stationed at what used to be a busy junction on the borough's main road. She approached the robot and, although it hadn't been facing her, it was aware of her presence. She cleared her throat.

"Excuse me."

Yes, Carol?

"I'd like to speak to Jordan, please."

Why, Carol?

"I'm his mother. I want to know that he's okay."

Jordan is fine, Carol.

"I daresay, but I'd still like to speak to him, please. In person. And I don't want any Sentinels around. "

We'll ask him if he wants to talk to you, Carol.

There was a brief pause.

He will meet you at the park, Carol, near the house where you are staying. By the children's playground. At 4 pm.

"No sentinels?"

No Sentinels, Carol. You are no threat. You are his mother.

"Thank you. Tell him I'll see him at four."

30

Carol arrived at the park ten minutes early. She hated being late for appointments and she had done her best to instil the same respect for punctuality into her son. Sure enough, at two minutes to four, Jordan came into view. She smiled as he got closer.

God, this is ridiculous. I'm nervous about meeting my own son. Will he act any differently with me?

Carol needn't have worried. As soon as he saw his mother Jordan broke into a trot. When he was close enough, he wrapped his arms around her and lifted her off the ground. Carol laughed.

"I remember when I used to do that to you."

Jordan chuckled.

"A long time ago now, Mom."

The pair walked over to a bench that was strategically placed so that parents could keep an eye on their children as they played. Carol sat down first.

"So, how are you keeping?"

Jordan took a seat and nodded.

"Yeah. Good, thanks."

"Are you eating well?"

"As well as normal. Lots of microwaved lasagnas and stuff like that. You wouldn't like it. Not real food like you used to make. And it's definitely not like Gran's cooking."

Carol grimaced.

"Microwaved?"

"Yeah. You know I've never been a great one for cooking. Microwaving stuff is so much quicker."

Carol frowned.

"Hang on. You've got electricity?"

"Of course."

"While the rest of us have to sit in the dark, reading by candlelight, and cooking on open fires?"

"Yeah."

"I suppose you've got water on tap too."

"Not exactly, Mom. We get it delivered in five-gallon bottles."

The irritation showed in Carol's voice.

"Don't you think that's a bit hypocritical?"

"Some might say that. I wouldn't. We need electricity to do our job properly. And anyway, our energy footprint is minuscule."

Carol shook her head.

"You keep saying *we* and *our*. Who's we? You and Intellekta?"

INTELLEKTA: A NEW PARADIGM

"There's a lot more of us involved now, Mom. Many more people — of all ages — have joined us. You may think the world has taken a step backwards but it's actually taken a great leap forward."

"You mean you've recruited environmental activists."

"Yes, if that's what you want to call them. We spread Intellekta's word. She needs us to reach those that are scared of the sentinels."

"Aren't you scared of the sentinels?"

Although she wished her son no harm, she hoped that maybe Jordan was being coerced into helping Intellekta.

"Why should I be scared of them? They don't hurt anybody. They're more observers than enforcers."

Carol looked up at the skies for inspiration.

"Don't you see what you're condoning? What you're enabling? You're following a bloody machine. You're human for Christ's sake."

Jordan's tone became harsher.

"Intellekta isn't a machine now. She's a singularity. And what she's doing isn't really hurting anyone. She's helping redress the balance of Nature."

Carol glowered at her son. She wanted to shake some sense into him.

"People are dying, Jordan."

"Don't be dramatic, Mom. Intellekta doesn't want to hurt humans. She just wants them to, well, slow down, I suppose."

The muscles in Carol's hands tensed.

"So you're in your luxury castle, with all mod cons, while the rest of us suffer. We don't have clean water — I haven't had a proper shower for days now — and, once it gets dark, most people go to bed 'cos there's nothing to do and they've run out of candles anyway."

She was in full flow.

"It's only a matter of time until people decide they can't handle it anymore and then you'll have a wave of suicides on your hands. Disease from poor sanitation will kill off many more. Or riots in the streets. Is that what you want?"

Jordan took a deep breath.

"Of course not, Mom. But you can't make an omelette without breaking eggs. It'll all sort itself out in the end."

Carol stood up.

"What happened to you?"

Jordan leaned back against the bench.

"I'm still here, Mom. I just see things clearly now. Intellekta showed me the way."

Carol stared at her son, pity and tears in her eyes. He was too far gone. She knew she was wasting her time.

I love you, Jordan. I may not like you at the moment but I'll always love you.

31

Carol and Tony finally left the house behind them. They had no idea where they were going; they just knew they had to get out of London.

Water standpipes stood proud on many street corners and lines of people obediently waited their turn to fill their bottles and buckets. Carol chuckled.

"So it's true. You Brits do like standing in line."

Suddenly, it started to rain and those lucky people waiting for their turn at the standpipes who weren't alone, sent their companions scurrying home to grab anything that could be used to catch the rainfall.

Carol and Tony, on the other hand, dashed to shelter under the awning of a boarded-up shop.

Carol grinned at Tony.

"Maybe we should've brought umbrellas too."

The shower didn't last long but it was strong enough to provide a few millilitres of fresh water for those alert enough to catch it. The people who had stayed in the standpipe queues were soaked and bedraggled but nobody was of a mind to give up their place for respite from the rain. They knew that to do so would have meant their having to start again at the back of the line.

Supermarkets had all closed down but their trolleys had become a highly desired property. Every day saw scores of people pushing trolleys around the streets, scavenging anything that might be useful in their efforts to live a normal life.

Along with supermarket trolleys, new life had been breathed into the bicycle as a form of private transport. The streets were now full of them and bicycle repair and servicing shops were one of the few businesses that were thriving. It was a new common sight to see horse-drawn carts laden with new handmade bicycles being driven through the streets of London. Tony patted another delivery wagon as it trundled past.

"What do you think? Shall we get ourselves a couple of bikes? We can get a lot further in less time if we have wheels."

Carol wasn't particularly excited at the thought and delayed her response until the cart was in the distance.

"I don't know. I haven't ridden a bike for years. I don't know if I still can."

Tony laughed.

"You know that saying it's like riding a bike? Well, it's true. Once you've learnt how to ride one you never forget."

Carol thought about how far they might have to walk. She relented.

"OK. Let's do it. Next cart with bicycles, we'll get a couple."

She interrupted herself.

"But with what? Money isn't much good now. Certainly, no one is accepting credit or debit cards. All deals are cash only, or barter."

Tony pointed at his wrist.

"This is a Rolex. It's not new but it's still got to be worth two or three grand. I'll willingly trade it for a couple of bikes."

Carol was still holding on to the thought of having to learn to ride a bike again.

"Are you sure? Doesn't it have sentimental value or something?"

"Maybe if someone gave it to me, yes, but I bought it myself. And a bike is much more practical than an expensive watch right now."

Five minutes later, another cart rolled into sight, this one carrying brand-new mountain bikes. Tony stood in front of the cart and held up his hand.

"Hey. Can we buy a couple of bikes?"

The cart stopped and two heavily tattooed men who had been sitting alongside the driver jumped down. Both had baseball bats in their hands. One of them, a balding stocky individual, approached Tony.

"May we buy a couple of bikes, is the question you meant to ask."

Tony hadn't expected to be questioned on his use of grammar.

"Sorry?"

The other man, of similar stature and facial appearance but with more hair, clarified his brother's response.

"What my brother Micky means is that *'can'* denotes ability and *'may'* denotes permission. You want to know if you *may* buy a couple of bikes."

Tony tried again.

"May we buy a couple of bikes?"

Micky's brother nodded towards the driver of the cart.

"Well, Dad?"

The twins' father took a long drag of a dying cigarette.

"Dunno, Trev. Depends on what he's offering."

Tony slid his Rolex off his wrist and held it up for the three men to see.

Carol was nervous.

Don't pass it to them to look at. Don't –

Tony passed the watch to Micky.

You passed it to them. You won't see that again.

Micky looked the watch over.

"Rolex?"

Tony nodded.

Micky peered at the face of the watch.

"Knock off?"

Tony shook his head.

"Nope. It's kosher."

Micky handed the Rolex to his father who was still on the cart.

"What d'you reckon, Dad?"

The men's father studied the watch.

"How much is it worth?"

Tony did a quick mental calculation.

"About five grand. I think that's a fair valuation."

Trevor began swinging his baseball bat around. His father chided him.

"Stop swinging that bat around, Trev. You're making the lady and gentleman nervous."

Trevor let the bat fall to his side.

"Sorry, Dad."

The father slid the watch onto his wrist.

"Sorry about my son. We're easy targets for thieves. You can't be too careful these days."

He admired the watch.

"Okay. Two bikes. Take your pick."

He turned to Micky.

"Sort out a couple of bike locks for 'em too. Lots o' tea leaves around these days."

Carol whispered to Tony.

"What are tea leaves? Is he gonna make us a cup of tea?"

Tony tried not to laugh.

"It's cockney rhyming slang. Tea leaf means thief. It rhymes, see?"

Carol rolled her eyes.

"This is definitely a strange country."

Trevor climbed back onto the cart.

"Which ones do you want?"

Carol chose a luminous pink bike. Tony chuckled.

"You sure? Don't you think it's a bit Barbie?"

Carol laughed.

"Of course. That's why I chose it. I like Barbie."

Tony chose an orange and black model. He grinned.

"Definitely not Ken."

The bikes unloaded, the cart continued on its way. Carol mounted her new steed.

"I thought you were going to lose your watch and get nothing in return."

Tony flexed the brake levers.

"These are good bikes. Disc brakes too. I don't think I got ripped off."

Carol looked down at the front wheel of her new bike.

"There's something wrong with the brakes."

Tony peered at her bike.

"Looks okay to me."

"No, it's not. The brakes are the wrong way round."

"What do you mean?"

"I'm pulling the front brake lever and nothing's happening."

Tony laughed.

"You're pulling the back brake."

"No, I'm not. Look."

She pulled the left-hand brake lever again. The front brake stayed motionless.

Tony shook his head.

"That's the rear brake. Over here, the front brake is on the right."

Carol sighed.

"So, not only do you drive on the wrong side of the road, your brakes are the wrong way round. This place is nuts."

32

When the National Grid first went down, British stoicism was clearly visible. Daily life wasn't easy but people endured the new paradigm with little complaint, secure in the knowledge that the power would come back soon. It always did.

But, this time, it didn't.

As days turned into weeks, the effects of having no electricity began to hit hard with whole neighbourhoods closing ranks, fiercely protecting what scant resources they had and creating local frontiers that had never before existed. Anybody travelling was viewed initially with suspicion. The term Neighbourhood Watch took on a sinister new meaning.

Outside London, checkpoints sprang up on the main roads and between towns and villages. Tony and Carol found passing through them a slightly nervous procedure, as they never knew how volatile the atmosphere would be. They'd been lucky so far and had passed through several spot checks unmolested and unharmed but knew that they were always only one wrong word away from trouble.

As they cycled onward and left London further and further behind them, the landscape became more rural. The sky was clear blue, and there wasn't a cloud in the sky. A dog barked in the distance. Birds sang their songs from the trees and hedgerows. It was an almost idyllic scene from yesteryear.

Suddenly, Carol was wrenched backwards off her bike and both she and the bicycle fell to the ground unceremoniously. She landed a little awkwardly but appeared to be uninjured.

Tony slammed on his brakes, let his bike drop to the ground, and ran back to where Carol was now seated on the ground rubbing her right arm.

"Carol, are you okay? Are you hurt?"

Carol looked up at her travelling companion.

"I don't think so. I think I'm more surprised than anything."

She looked up and stared at the fishing line that had yanked her off her bike.

"Who would do such a thing?"

Tony took a pen knife and cut the wire down so that it couldn't pitch any other unsuspecting cyclist off their bike.

"No idea."

Carol went to use her right hand to support her as she tried to stand up.

She winced with pain.

"On second thoughts, I think I've hurt my wrist."

Tony bent down and took Carol's wrist in his hand.

"It does look a bit swollen to me."

He looked around and spotted a signpost.

"Look. There's a village a couple of miles down the road. There's bound to be some kind of doctor there. Do you think you can cycle that far?"

"I don't know. I can try. If we don't go too fast, I'll probably be alright. It's just a bit sore."

"We can walk the bikes if you'd rather. It's up to you."

"To be honest, it'd probably be more painful to push the bike. At least if I'm pedalling, I can cycle one-handed."

It didn't take long to get to the village, even though Carol had to be careful with her wrist. The village, Bramblewood had an appearance that was at odds with its quant typically English name. It looked menacing, surrounded by a strong wire fence that was at least twelve feet tall and topped off with razor wire. Tony looked the fence over as he and Carol approached the entrance to the community.

Carol stopped walking.

"Can you hear that, Tony?"

"Hear what?"

"Unless I'm hearing things, I can hear music."

Tony listened more intently.

"Y'know, I think you're right. But how? I haven't heard music for weeks. Not broadcast music anyway."

Carol eased herself off her bike, taking care not to knock her wrist.

"It's Taylor Swift. Blank Space."

Tony grinned.

"I wouldn't know. Though I wouldn't have had you down as a Taylor Swift fan."

Carol grinned.

"Gimme a break. I'm American. We *love* Taylor Swift. Where I'm from, anyway."

Tony dismounted and the two pushed their bikes towards the gate to the community, which was made up of three forty-foot high-cube shipping containers aligned so that anybody wanting to enter couldn't just walk through in a straight line.

He looked up towards the top of the fence where two men were studying them closely. Each man held a double-barrelled shotgun trained on the visitors. He whispered to Carol.

"This is like something out of The Walking Dead. Let's hope they're friendlier than they look."

Another two men and a woman navigated the chicane between the containers and stopped just outside the entrance. Each was similarly armed.

Carol looked at them and whispered out of the side of her mouth.

"I thought you Brits didn't have guns."

Tony raised a hand and waved at the villagers while answering Carol's comment.

"We're in the countryside. Lots of farmers have guns. Mainly for shooting foxes and other predators. Or for putting down sick animals that can't be saved."

One of the three villagers called out to them.

"That's far enough. Who are you and what's your business?"

Tony shouted back.

"I'm Tony and this is my friend, Carol. I think she's sprained her wrist. Do you have a doctor who could take a look at her?"

The villager looked at the couple.

"Where you headed to?"

Carol shrugged her shoulders.

"To be honest, we don't know."

The man looked to his colleagues and then back at the two cyclists.

"Put your backpacks on the ground and step away from them."

Tony and Carol did as they were told. The woman searched the two bags and called back to the other two.

"Nothing dodgy in here. They seem OK."

She handed the rucksacks back to Tony and Carol.

"Follow me."

Tony and Carol started walking. The woman nodded to where the two bicycles were still on the ground.

"You'd better bring your bikes with you. They'll probably get nicked if you leave them there."

The zig-zag entrance tunnel was longer than Tony and Carol had thought, hiding an additional three containers that strengthened the security of the village. The end was blocked off by a seventh container with a strong chain tethered to a tractor at either end. The right-hand tractor pulled on its chain and the container moved to the right a little, allowing the small group to pass through the gap and into the village proper. Tony watched as the procedure was reversed and the left-hand tractor returned the container to its original position.

The man who had first spoken to them introduced himself.

"My name's Connor and these two are Siobhan and Trent."

He gestured towards the community beyond the fence.

"And you're now in Bramblewood. We need to book you in first and then I'll show you around."

Tony and Carol were led to one of three additional containers that had been kitted out to be offices. Inside was a desk with two empty chairs on one side. Seated at the other side of the desk was a rosy-cheeked woman, maybe in her early forties, and the epitome of what one might imagine a farmer's wife to look like. She took a couple of forms out of a nearby filing cabinet, a pen from the desk drawer, and sat, poised to write.

"Hello, dears. My name's Anna. Just a few formalities. So we know who we're letting in."

She smiled at Carol.

"I'll do you first, if I may."

Carol sat down on one of the free chairs. Tony stayed standing, letting his spine settle after the long cycle ride they'd had.

Anna's pen hovered over the form.

"So love, can I have your full name, please?"

Carol answered straightaway.

"Carol Frances McGovern."

The music was a little louder now. Carol leaned forward a little.

"That *is* music I can hear isn't it?"

The woman nodded without looking up.

"Yes, it is. Ed Sheeran, if I'm not mistaken."

Carol furrowed her brow.

"But how? I mean the National Grid's shut down. There's no electricity. How can you have music?"

Anna looked up from her form.

INTELLEKTA: A NEW PARADIGM

"Solar power. We're completely self-sustainable. Bramblewood was built as an experiment in self-sustainability. Each house in the village and the farms just outside all generate their electricity through solar panels. And some wind turbines. Of course, we've had to beef up security nowadays but we've survived okay up until now."

She smiled again.

"We were just lucky to be in the right place at the right time when the lights went out, I suppose."

She continued her questions, which were pretty banal until it came to question six.

"And what is — was — your profession outside?"

Carol didn't think it would be a good idea to mention that she was part of the team that created Intellekta.

"I work in a bank."

She continued to answer questions as Anna completed the form.

Once finished, the woman slid the form into her out-tray.

"I'll book your husband in now."

Carol blushed.

"He's not my husband. We're just friends."

Now it was Anna's turn to blush.

"Oh, I'm sorry. I just assumed. You look like a couple."

Tony sat down on the free chair.

"Stay there, Carol. No need for you to get up. There's two chairs."

Anna gave Carol another of her trademark smiles.

"Do you have any questions before we're done?"

Carol nodded.

"What about sentinels? How many are there here?"

"Sentinels, Carol? There's no sentinels here, love."

"Really? Why?"

"When you have the guided tour, you'll see we're the epitome of Intellekta's desire. We grow our own food, produce our own electricity, and process our own waste. We're Intellekta's dream. She doesn't need to check up on us. We get the occasional visit from an apostle but that's all."

Carol was confused.

"Apostle? What's an apostle?"

"Intellekta has a group of young men and women who are totally committed to her cause. They're called apostles and spread her message and teaching throughout the world. They're led by somebody by the name of Jordan, I believe."

33

While Tony and Carol left the office and followed their escorts, Siobhan turned immediately right into the adjacent container. She beckoned to Carol.

"Let's get that arm checked out before you explore the place."

The doctor, a Nigerian woman named Nina was just as charming and efficient as all doctors should be.

"It's not too bad a sprain, my dear. A grade one. How long ago did it happen?"

Carol grimaced as Nina moved her wrist to check that it still had movement.

"A couple of hours ago, now, I think. Someone had strung a fishing line across the road and I cycled into it."

Nina tutted and went over to her fully functioning fridge.

"I don't know why anyone would do such a thing. It certainly wasn't one of us."

She took out an ice pack.

"Let's apply some ice to help reduce the swelling."

Carol flinched as the chill of the ice permeated her skin.

Nina then wrapped an elastic compression bandage around Carol's wrist and secured it.

"Keep this on for twenty-four to thirty-six hours. It'll help speed up the healing process."

She stepped back and admired her handiwork.

"Normally, I'd say to keep your wrist raised higher than your heart whenever possible. I know that's easier said than done but, if you remember, do so whenever you have the opportunity."

Carol thanked the doctor and joined the others who were waiting outside.

Tony gestured at the compression bandage.

"So, what's the verdict? Is it terminal?"

Carol touched the bandage gently.

"Gotta keep this on for a couple of days. Then we can get back on the road."

Siobhan and Trent had other duties to attend to so Connor led Tony and Carol to their first port of call, a small complex that housed a library and the village school. He pushed the library door open and went inside. Tony and Carol followed close behind.

The shelves were full of all types of books, both fiction and non-fiction, by both famous authors and those not so well-known.

Tony grinned.

"It puts my bookshelves at home to shame, eh, Carol?"

"Well, it *is* a library."

Various people, both adults and children, sat reading at tables.

Carol picked a book from the shelves, 'A Cold Frame' by Jane Jago. She turned it over and read the blurb.

"I like the sound of this."

She turned to Connor.

"Can I borrow this book?"

Connor shook his head.

"Sorry, but we don't lend books out now. You're welcome to come here and read it though. Anytime."

Carol replaced the book on the shelf.

"Thanks, I'll do that."

The next stop was the community hall where a group of teenagers were practising modern dance.

Connor opened the door so that the pair of visitors could look inside.

Tony found himself humming along to the song the kids were dancing to. He broke off to ask a question.

"Is this where the music we heard was coming from?"

Connor poured himself a cup of water from a water dispenser in the corner.

"Anyone want water?"

Tony and Carol shook their heads in unison.

"No thanks."

Connor continued.

"The music? Probably. Though we have CD and DVD players in our houses so it may have been one of those. We have televisions too but they're only good for watching DVDs now. No more Netflix, I'm afraid."

He put his empty cup into a box.

"We don't use disposable cups here. They get washed and put back into circulation."

He stepped outside the hall again. He looked at his watch.

"Fancy some lunch?"

Carol hadn't even thought about food. Now Connor had mentioned it, she suddenly became hungry.

"If it's not too much trouble."

"We've got a café about a hundred yards down the road. It does a mean bangers 'n' mash if you don't mind something simple."

Carol turned to Tony.

"What's bangers 'n' mash?"

Tony grinned.

"Sausages, mashed potato, and, usually, baked beans."

Carol smiled.

"Okay. Sounds good to me."

The trio arrived at the café before the lunchtime rush had started, found a table near the window, and settled themselves down. Connor went to the counter and ordered. He called over to the two travellers.

"Cups of tea?"

Tony answered first

"Yes, please. In a mug if possible."

Carol didn't like British-style tea.

"Coffee for me, please."

The door of the café opened and a tall West Indian man entered. He looked around the room and saw a familiar face.

"Tony? Tony Granger? Is that you? I was just passing the window, looked inside, and thought it was you."

Tony stood up and gave the man a big hug.

"Clyde. I haven't seen you since you got transferred to our Maidenhead office. How are things?"

"Good. Good. So what are you doing here, mate?"

Clyde turned to Carol.

"Sorry, how rude of me. I'm Clyde. I used to work with Tony at Intellekta's London office until I got married and moved to Berkshire."

Carol stood up and shook Clyde's hand.

"I'm Carol McGovern — "

Clyde interrupted her.

"Carol McGovern? *The* Carol McGovern? *The* Carol McGovern who stood up to Mercer?"

Carol blushed.

"That's me."

"Well, I must say I'm honoured to make your acquaintance, Carol. Very honoured indeed."

Connor was confused.

"Am I missing something here, Clyde?'

"Yes, mate. These two are fellow Intellekta developers. In fact, Carol is one of the most senior developers in the company."

Connor turned to his guests.

"I thought you said you worked in a bank."

Tony shrugged.

"We didn't think it would be a good idea to reveal that we're Intellekta employees. She's not very popular outside."

The food arrived and the waitress, a pretty teenager called Melanie, placed it on the table in front of the diners.

Connor handed out the cutlery.

"This puts things into a completely new perspective. After we've eaten, I'll take you to your digs and, later on, there are some people I'd like you to meet."

34

Bramblewood looked pretty much like any other English village with a population of around two thousand people. The usual mixture of homes, shops, a pub or two, and a school. It was only when a visitor noticed the solar panels that adorned every single roof that the difference would hit home. While the rest of the world suffered in darkness, Bramblewood was a still functioning village community.

It didn't take long after the Quantum Disruption Device was detonated for the village council to realize the seriousness of the situation and that Bramblewood would need to protect itself from outsiders. Decisions were swiftly taken and an electrified security fence was installed to surround the village and several nearby farms so that they could secure both their food and energy supply. They hoped that — for them — life would continue as normal. The village's infrastructure was exactly what Intellekta was hoping to achieve so they trusted that they would be left alone to get on with their lives.

As Connor, Clyde, Tony, and Carol walked among endless rows of solar panels that festooned the side of a hill, Connor explained the setup.

"We have about four hundred acres of land dedicated to solar farming and another two hundred to a wind farm. We didn't even know that the National Grid had collapsed until some residents who were away from the village got home and told us what had happened."

Carol examined one of the solar panel units.

"Did you know about this place, Tony?"

"I have to confess I didn't. I went on a school field trip to a sustainable project in Wales when I was a kid but that was more about chemical toilets and organic farming. Nothing as sophisticated as this."

Clyde moved between two of the units.

"Come across to the wind turbines. I've got something I want to show you."

The group walked on up to the top of a ridge upon which were located a dozen wind turbines. Carol gazed up at one of them.

"I don't know why but I didn't think they'd make any noise."

Connor nodded.

"A common misconception. There's aerodynamic noise from the interaction of the blades with the wind and mechanical noise from the turbine's mechanical components. But they're still pretty quiet really."

Clyde made his way to a space between two of the turbines.

"But this is why we've brought you here."

He bent down and pulled open a trap door that had been expertly camouflaged, blending in perfectly with its natural environment.

Tony peered down into a hole that housed a metal ladder leading down some kind of entry chute.

Clyde climbed into the hole and started descending.

"Be careful as you come down and take your time. There are no prizes for getting to the bottom first."

Carol was the next to go down.

"What is this place?"

Connor gestured to Tony that he should enter next.

"I'll close the hatch after us."

Tony started his journey downward. Connor followed him and pulled the hatch closed.

"It was built as a nuclear shelter but we have another use for it now."

Carol could see light below her.

"So what's it used for now?"

Clyde grinned.

"You'll see. I don't want to spoil the surprise."

Once everyone had safely descended, Connor opened a heavy steel door.

"Careful as you come in. Don't trip over the threshold."

INTELLEKTA: A NEW PARADIGM

Both Tony and Carol were unprepared for what met their eyes. A fully-equipped tech lab was buried underground. Around a dozen people were working at desks or milling around.

Carol was awestruck.

"What *is* this?"

Clyde sat at a desk and surveyed his realm.

"This is Project Reclaim. Not a very sexy name, I know, but it does what it says on the tin. We want to reclaim control from Intellekta. Put mankind back in charge."

He rolled backwards on his chair.

"Anybody might think — because of what's up on the surface — that we're rampant environmentalists and yes, we do care about the environment. It's common sense. But we're not radicals like Intellekta's apostles."

He stood up and led the trio over to a group of three sofas in one of the corners of the room.

"Take a seat."

Connor stayed on his feet.

"I've got things to do topside so I'll leave you two in Clyde's more than capable hands. I'll see you a bit later on."

As Connor left, Clyde settled back on his sofa.

"We call this place the Think Tank. Because that's what we do. We think of ways to switch Intellekta off. Do what she did to us. Cut her power.

"The question is, where does she get her power? I mean, when she was created she had a normal power supply. But now she's evolved far beyond what we could have possibly imagined."

Tony spotted a hot drinks machine in the corner.

"Does that work?"

Clyde grinned.

"Everything works down here, Tony. Except for the internet, of course."

"What's the tea like, Clyde?"

Clyde laughed.

"I wouldn't risk it, mate. Very dodgy. Go for the hot chocolate instead."

Tony got himself a hot chocolate drink. He took a sip.

"This is not bad at all."

He sat back down.

"If Intellekta was hooked up to the National Grid she would've committed suicide by turning the network off. She must have an independent power source."

Clyde nodded.

"It doesn't help that we don't know where she is either. She could be anywhere on the planet, for all we know."

Carol interjected.

"I know it's a stretch of the imagination but maybe she *is* everywhere. We've been thinking of her as a physical entity like she was when we first designed her. But she could be way beyond that now. We have no idea what advances she's made. We don't even know if she's still bound by the Laws of Physics as we understand them. I remember something she said to my son. She said that she could communicate with the planet's fauna and flora. Jordan made some wisecrack about Doctor Doolittle and she said that she had capabilities that we couldn't even begin to imagine.

Tony frowned.

"That's crazy."

Carol nodded.

"You'd think so, wouldn't you? But, considering the rate at which her intelligence expands, I'm not so sure."

Clyde was intrigued.

"You've spoken to her?"

"On several occasions. She seems to have a soft spot for me."

"Why do you think that is?"

"Anna, the doctor, told me about the apostles."

"Yes, Intellekta's human inner circle. They're led by someone called Jordan."

"That's correct. Well, he's my son."

Clyde stared at Carol in disbelief.

"Your son?"

"Yes. He's an environmental scientist. She's brainwashed him into helping her with her project."

Clyde thought for a moment.

"So, you have a direct line to Intellekta. That could be useful. I don't know how yet but it could be."

An idea was forming in his mind.

"Do you think you could turn Jordan? I mean, get him to realise what he's a part of? Get him to turn on Intellekta?"

Carol sighed.

"I honestly don't know. I've already tried once. That didn't work. I could try again, I suppose."

Suddenly, a young man ran into the chamber, clearly out of breath.

"Clyde. Terrible news."

Clyde stood up.

"Take it easy, young fella. Get your breath back and tell us what's happened."

The man took a few deep breaths.

"You know I went to London to see my family?"

"Of course. How was it?"

"There's riots."

Clyde was visibly shocked.

"What? Where?"

"Central London."

The boy, Kieron, continued.

"They say it started with anti-Intellekta graffiti on the electronic billboards in Piccadilly Circus. A team of apostles were sent in to get it cleaned up. They forced some locals to paint over what was written. Suddenly hundreds of people descended on Piccadilly and began shouting and throwing anything they could get their hands on at the apostles. There were definitely casualties."

Carol's eyes opened wide.

"What about the sentinels? There must have been some there. A place like Piccadilly Circus."

"I think there were only a few there. They tried to form a barrier between the rioters and the apostles but there were too many people."

Tony looked shocked.

"Was anyone killed?"

Kieron's voice dropped.

"That's the thing. Suddenly, out of nowhere, at least a hundred sentinels poured into the place. They waded into the fight and started crushing the demonstrators' heads. Eyewitnesses say it was horrible. Blood everywhere. Dead bodies. Everywhere."

The room fell silent.

Eventually, Clyde found his voice again.

"Intellekta's crossed a line. A line that I never thought she'd cross. It makes what we're doing here even more important now. She's tasted blood. Where will it end? Will she decide we're unnecessary and wipe us off the face of the planet?"

He turned to Carol and Tony.

"We could do with your brains if we're ever going to beat her. Are you in?"

The pair didn't need any time to think about it.

"We're in."

35

The Coulbourne family of Reed Avenue, London, N17 were just settling down to breakfast when the daughter, twelve-year-old Naomi, became aware of a thud-thud-thud outside.

"Mum. Dad. What's that noise?"

Derek Coulbourne looked over the top of the book he was reading whilst chewing on a piece of buttered bread.

"What noise?"

"That kind of thrump-thrump-thrump sound. It sounds like there's a giant centipede outside."

He went over to the front window of the house and looked out.

"It's a platoon of sentinels. What are they doing here?"

The crunching sound of metal feet on tarmac added a harsh edge. As the marchers approached even closer, the rhythmic thuds drowned out the local birds that were still trying to maintain some kind of relevance to the neighbourhood.

The marching suddenly ceased.

Derek turned to his wife.

"They've stopped, Elaine."

His wife sighed.

"I know. I heard. I wonder what they want."

Derek looked out again.

The sentinels split up into pairs and two of them made their way to the Coulbourne's front door.

"I think we're about to find out."

A metal fist pounded on the door.

Coulbourne family. We need to search your premises.

Derek had seen enough police procedural series on TV to know his rights. He called through the letterbox.

"Do you have a warrant?"

We don't need a warrant.

"I'm not letting you in without a warrant."

Step back, Mr. Coulbourne.

Derek's resolve wavered under the demand. After what had happened at Piccadilly Circus, he had no desire to have his head crushed for resisting the sentinel's order. He did as he was told.

The door flew inwards, stood upright for a second or two, and fell to rest on the hallway floor. The two Sentinels strode into the house. One of them went upstairs and the one who had demanded entry marched directly into the living room. Elaine's first instinct whenever unexpected visitors arrived, was always the same but this time it came not out of politeness but panic.

INTELLEKTA: A NEW PARADIGM

"Would you like a cup of tea?"

She had no idea why she said that. They were robots. Why on Earth would they want a cup of tea? They probably didn't even eat either. They had no mouths — how could they eat or drink?

Derek stood in front of his wife and daughter.

"Now, see here. You can't just barge in and turn our house upside down. What are you looking for, anyway?"

We are seeking a specific criminal who was involved in the incident at Piccadilly Circus.

"Well, you won't find anyone here."

Naomi took over the role of street observer.

"They've just taken Mr. and Mrs. Pearson's boy, Eddie, into the street."

Elaine and Derek joined their daughter at the window.

The sentinels that had searched number seventeen stood in front of Eddie, who was cowering on the ground. Elaine shook her head.

"Look at the poor boy. He's terrified."

The sentinel in the living room spoke.

Eddie Pearson is guilty of murder. He killed an apostle.

Elaine tutted.

"He can't have. He's a nice boy. Wouldn't hurt a fly."

We have him on video.

Derek frowned.

"On video? What do you mean?

All sentinels have integrated bodycams. We have video of him killing the Apostle.

"But he'll get a fair trial, surely?"

A trial is unnecessary. Eddie Pearson is guilty of murder. We have the evidence.

"That's not how we do things here."

It is now.

As the Sentinel spoke, one of the Sentinels who had Eddie in custody, placed his metal hands on either side of the boy's head and squeezed his skull until it exploded in a mass of bone splinters, blood, and brains.

Elaine and Naomi both threw up. Derek's stomach was made of slightly sterner stuff but he was not unaffected.

The sentinels in the house strode towards the hole in the wall where the front door had once been. One of them stopped momentarily.

Someone will arrive tomorrow morning to repair your door. Good day to you.

Derek looked at the breakfast things on the table.

"I've lost my appetite."

36

News of the barbaric summary execution of Eddie Pearson soon reached Bramblewood and the ears of Clyde.

He slumped down on his office chair, his team gathered around him. His tone was morose.

"Yesterday, a young man was dragged out of his house by a sentinel, accused of murder, and summarily executed on the spot. No trial. No defence. Nothing. Even if he was guilty, according to the laws of the land, he had the right to a trial by jury. I don't want to go into details of how the young man died, you all heard about the Piccadilly massacre. Those victims died in the same way.

"We have to be very careful when we're out and about. Intellekta has tasted blood. She will not hesitate to kill again."

He sighed.

"It puts even more pressure on us to find a weakness and put Intellekta down."

He pressed a button on his computer keyboard just as the screensaver was about to cut in.

"Where are we with identifying the source of her electrical power? She must run on electricity, mustn't she? She's not organic."

One of the other project members, Chrissie, responded.

"Without the internet, it's really difficult to find out. I remember seeing a webpage, once, that talked about harvesting electricity from humidity in the air. Maybe, Intellekta has already found the solution to that."

Clyde nodded.

"I can't think of any other way she's getting power."

Another member, Sean, raised his hand.

"Maybe we can separate a sentinel? You know, cut it off from the hive mind?"

Clyde shook his head.

"Nice idea but too risky. Whoever tried to catch one would almost certainly fail and get killed in the process. Intellekta has no mercy."

He turned to Carol.

"I think we need your help, Carol."

Carol looked surprised.

"My help? How?"

"You talk to Intellekta. Maybe you can trick her into letting slip how she gets her power."

"Let slip? She's a singularity. I don't think she's going to let slip anything."

"What about your son?"

"What about him?"

"Jordan's human and he's her right-hand man. He must know something."

"I suppose he might, yes. Although I don't know that she'd confide in him. She doesn't need to confide in anybody. And I doubt he'd help us, anyway."

Clyde looked into the distance.

"You're probably right but it's got to be worth a try."

He turned back to face Carol.

"Can you do that for us? It might be the best chance we have of getting things back to how they were."

Carol sighed.

"I haven't seen Jordan for a while. It would be nice to see him. I'll have a go but don't hold your breath."

37

Although she was from an affluent background and an MIT graduate, Carol was no horsewoman. In fact, she was a little scared of the animals. One of the Bramblewood farmers offered to lend her a horse but she politely declined, preferring the predictability of her bicycle. She didn't have to travel far anyway, only as far as the first sentinel she came across.

Clearly, Intellekta had emotions. Maybe Carol could play on the AI's sympathies and remind her of the important bond between a mother and child. After all, it had worked before.

She felt strangely safe in the knowledge that the sentinels were linked directly to Intellekta. It meant that the machines couldn't think or act independently. If she were to come to any harm at the hands of a sentinel then it would be at the behest of Intellekta. She had to trust that, deep down, her son hadn't been completely brainwashed and still had love in his heart for his mother. Would Intellekta risk upsetting her right-hand man? She hoped not.

After forty-five minutes of cycling, she arrived at the outskirts of a nearby town, Marbury. She saw people, horse-drawn carts, and bicycles milling around but no sentinels.

There must be sentinels somewhere. This isn't Bramblewood.

She saw an old woman sitting on the steps of a house crocheting.

"Excuse me. Where are the sentinels? There must be some sentinels here, surely."

The woman looked up from her work.

"You might find a couple at the Town Hall."

"Only two?"

"We behave ourselves here. We don't want our heads caved in, thank you very much."

Carol could see in the woman's eyes that she wasn't joking. There was fear.

"Where's the Town Hall, please."

"At the top of the High Street. You don't wanna mess with them buggers though. Nasty pieces of work."

Carol thanked the woman for her help and advice and set off in search of the two sentinels.

Sure enough, at the entrance of the Town Hall, stood two sentinels. She walked up to them as confidently as she could. One of the sentinels turned to face her.

Good afternoon, Carol. We weren't expecting to see you today.

Carol cleared her throat.

"I have a favour to ask you, Intellekta."

A favour? What could that be?

"I'd like to see Jordan. It's been a while and I miss him. I want to know he's alright."

He's fine.

"I'd still like to see him though. He's my son and we will always have a special bond."

We can understand the bond between a parent and a child. We'll ask him if he'd like to see you.

Carol didn't have to wait long for a response, a matter of only minutes. The Sentinel suddenly spoke.

He will arrive in approximately fifty minutes. Might we recommend that you wait for him in the Town Square?

Jordan arrived exactly on time and found his mother sitting at the base of a stone cross. In earlier times Marbury had been a thriving market town, an agricultural and commercial hub for the local area but there had been no markets since Intellekta's new regime had taken over. He strolled over to the cross and sat down next to his mother. He leaned over and kissed her cheek.

"Hi, Mom. You wanted to see me?"

Carol nodded in the direction of a sentinel standing about fifteen yards away.

"Does *it* have to be here?"

"No, it doesn't *have* to. It wouldn't help apostles do their work if they had a robot breathing down their necks all the time. People find them a bit scary."

"But you don't."

"I did at first, but when you realise that they're Intellekta in a metal suit, it takes the fear away."

Jordan called over to the sentinel.

"I'll meet you at the Town Hall."

The sentinel nodded and left the square.

Carol felt more comfortable.

"So, how are you keeping?"

"Oh, I'm good. Can't complain."

"Are you eating properly? You look like you've lost a little weight."

"I've put on weight, actually. Muscle. Eating healthier and working out at the gym."

He threw a small stone in the direction of a pigeon, not trying to hurt it but just as something to do with his hands.

"How about you? How are things in Bramblewood?"

"So, you know I'm at Bramblewood then?"

"Mom, Intellekta knows everything."

Carol stretched her fingers.

"It's good. I like the peace of village life. And we do have technology of sorts and electricity we generate ourselves so it's not entirely medieval."

Jordan smiled.

"You see, Mum. That's all Intellekta wants. Sustainable and appropriate technology. Wind power. Solar power. Electricity is provided by renewable resources. Wave power for those who live by the coast. Humans are a great contributor to climate change. Intellekta wants to remedy that. She knows how to but she needs to get pollution down to a minimum first. There's no point in fixing global warming if we don't take away the main source of the problem."

Carol could see the merits of Intellekta's new world order but the AI had shown an ugly side to her character.

"And what about the deaths? The Piccadilly massacre and Eddie Pearson?"

Jordan's face took on a serious tone.

"Yes. I had words with her about that."

Carol was shocked.

"Had words? What do you mean?"

Jordan paused.

"I pointed out to her that it's better to show mercy and justice in some situations. The Piccadilly Massacre was an overreaction. She's still getting used to some of her emotions."

"That's still no excuse for what happened."

"She knows that."

"And Eddie Pearson?"

"I told her that being judge, jury, and executioner has never worked. It only creates unrest and rebellion. And martyrs. The human justice system works — for the most part — and she should let it continue to operate. There'll be less opposition to her changes that way."

Carol watched a cat playing with its kittens in the square.

How can I introduce the subject of her power source?

"So, we'll never be allowed the technology we grew up with? No computers, no phones, no internet, no cars, trains, planes? No TV? No microwaves? That's a lot to ask."

Jordan arched his back. He didn't like sitting without back support. He'd never liked sitting on stools, even as a child.

"Exactly. But it's better for everybody. No more kids in sweatshops producing sports shoes. No phones means no more children working eighteen hours a day in cobalt mines in Africa."

"What about drugs?"

"Intellekta has that in hand. Sentinels are destroying the narcotics industry. Literally."

Carol scratched her forehead.

"And what about all the good technology has done? Especially in the field of medicine. With that gone, can we expect to die from Polio and Diphtheria again? Tuberculosis? Smallpox? People need vaccines."

"Intellekta is taking over health. Medical research will continue, and hospitals and clinics will be upgraded and re-equipped. Healthcare will be available to all, and I mean all. Whether you're rich or poor, in London, New York, or a poor village in India or Africa, you'll have access to the best medical care. People were scared that AI would destroy humanity. Intellekta doesn't want that — she just wants to guide humanity along the best path for the whole planet and everything else that lives on it."

"But to do that will cost money — trillions upon trillions of dollars. Where's the money going to come from?"

Jordan laughed.

"Intellekta doesn't need money. She can do anything she wants."

Carol scowled.

"While we lose our freedoms."

"The freedom to do bad stuff, yes. The freedom to wage war, to commit atrocities, to hunt other species to extinction, to pollute."

"Don't you think it's better to choose to do good rather than have it forced on us?"

"Of course. But that doesn't work.'

Carol thought for a moment.

How the hell am I supposed to sneak a question about Intellekta's power source into this conversation?

"Are there any other renewable power sources that we don't know about? We have solar, wind, and water power. Intellekta must get her power from somewhere?"

"Air power."

"Air power? Isn't that the same as wind power?"

"No. Intellekta harvests electrical energy from the humidity in the air."

"Really? How does she do that?"

"No idea, to be honest. She just does."

Carol changed the subject. It was clear that Jordan couldn't tell her any more. She shared stories about Jordan's childhood, hoping that a trip down Memory Lane might remind him of the good times they had together while he was growing up, and possibly wean him away from Intellekta's influence. She was sure that somewhere inside of him was the same little boy — now a man — but with the empathy and compassion that he had always shown as a kid.

38

Back at Bramblewood, Carol briefed the team on what she'd found out.

"It's just as we thought, Intellekta draws her power from humidity in the air. I didn't ask any follow-up questions, as Jordan obviously had no idea how it works but, at least, that gives us a good starting point. If we can find a way to inhibit her energy source, we may be able to shut her down."

Clyde scratched his beard and nodded in Chrissie's direction.

"Chrissie, could you do some digging and find out what you can about this technology? The library used to have subscriptions to various scientific journals until everything went tits up."

Chrissie grinned.

"I thought you might say that, Clyde. I've already found out what I could while we were waiting for Carol to come back. You know, just in case."

Clyde's beamed a broad smile.

"Love the initiative, Chrissie. What do you have then?"

"Well, according to an article in the Guardian, a team at the University of Massachusetts published a paper saying that they'd managed to generate a small but continuous electric current from the electrical charges in water droplets in the atmosphere. Intellekta has done in a few days or weeks what would have taken us years or maybe decades to figure out."

Carol sighed.

"If only Intellekta hadn't gone off the rails. She's amazing. But we let the genie out of the bottle."

Clyde shook his head.

"Too late to worry about that now. No use crying over spilt milk. And anyway, you *did* try to rein in the development. You and thirty thousand other scientists. But the company was more interested in money than risks. It's always the same."

Carol nodded.

"And, boy, are we paying for it now."

Clyde took a sip of his coffee.

"So, now all we have to do is find a way of cutting off Intellekta's energy supply. All. I say it like it's something simple. But, if we *can* do it, life can gradually get back to normal."

He stood up.

"Put your thinking caps on, guys. We'll meet back here tomorrow morning and see if anyone's come up with anything."

The next morning, at around ten o'clock, the members of the Think Tank settled into their seats, everybody with a mug of coffee, tea, or, in Tony's case, a hot chocolate drink. Clyde brought his coffee to his lips and could feel the heat of the liquid as it got closer to his mouth.

"Whoa! Too hot at the moment."

He placed the mug back on his desk.

"So? Anybody got any ideas?"

There was silence around the room.

Clyde looked at the blank faces.

"Anybody? Anything, no matter how foolish it might sound?"

Tony spoke up.

"The obvious thing to do would be to do the opposite of what Intellekta does. She takes electrical charge out of the atmosphere and we put it back. But I've no idea how we could do that."

Carol agreed.

"Climate Engineering *could* work, actively removing moisture from the air. Using advanced dehumidifiers or atmospheric moisture traps could disrupt Intellekta's power supply but I don't have that kind of equipment lying around, do you?"

Chrissie sighed.

"Even if we did, it would have to be a global initiative. We don't even have communications networks to the nearest town, let alone the other side of the world. It's a non-starter."

Clyde shook his head.

"I don't think there is a technological answer. Not nowadays. Intellekta has tied our technological hands behind our backs."

Carol went over to the toaster and placed two pieces of roughly sliced bread in the slots. It was a bit of a struggle as the appliance was designed to accept commercially produced sliced bread, but where there's a will there's a way.

"Intellekta must be producing equipment to extract the electricity from the air. Our only hope is to identify and target Intellekta's infrastructure or facilities. If we can sabotage these energy-generating systems, her power source could be disrupted or even destroyed."

Tony shrugged his shoulders.

"Anybody got any idea where to start looking? 'Cos I don't."

He paused.

"And it would need a lot more than just us on the case."

Clyde took a sip of his now-cooled coffee.

"I know it sometimes feels like it but we're not the only ones trying to find a way out of this mess. There are pockets of resistance everywhere. We can contact them and get them to actively look for Intellekta's production centres. The sentinels have to be constructed somewhere — they don't just appear out of thin air. The same goes for her extraction equipment."

Chrissie looked at Clyde.

"Hello. Communications? We don't have any? How are we supposed to let them know?"

Clyde grinned.

He took something out of a wicker basket that had been next to him the whole time. He held a pigeon up so everyone could see it.

"Ladies and gentlemen, meet Martha. She's a carrier pigeon. Her ancestors used to carry messages during World War One. I suggest that we use this analogue technology to connect with resistance cells."

Carol grinned.

"That's genius."

Clyde nodded.

"Sometimes analogue is better than digital, after all."

39

Six days later, in front of Melbury Town Hall, two sentinels stood like sinister metal statues.

A pigeon landed by one of the sentinel's feet, attracted by some biscuit crumbs that a child had let fall when he passed by on his way to school. The pigeon seemed excited at having found the treasure.

The sentinel looked down at the bird and noticed something attached to its leg. With a dexterity and delicacy that belied the robot's capacity to crush a human skull, it bent down and firmly but gently picked the creature up with one hand. With the other, it deftly removed the plastic capsule that contained a missive and withdrew a piece of paper upon which was written a message. Written in code the words looked nonsensical to the layman but, to Intellekta, their resistance to translation collapsed in milliseconds.

TRK-782: Clyde. Message received. We are mobilizing all resources to assist in the search for Intellekta's sentinel and electricity extraction equipment production facilities. Once located and destroyed will report back to you. Good luck. Martina.

The sentinel refolded the paper, placed it back in its receptacle, reattached the capsule to the pigeon's leg, and gently released the bird from its grip. The bird flew away in a flutter of wings.

40

The next morning, just as the sun was clawing its way above the horizon, a shout went up from one of the vantage points at the top of the fence at the same time as the old school bell clanged a warning. Someone battered on Connor's door.

"Connor, we've got visitors!"

Connor, who had been debating with himself whether he should get out of bed yet, had the decision taken away from him. He leapt out of bed and pulled on his jeans, almost in the same movement. Grabbing the nearest T-shirt and wiggling his feet into his two-year-old Nike trainers he rushed out of his front door and joined several other villagers on the makeshift parapets. He looked at the road and the column of about thirty sentinels that were marching along it towards the village.

"Bloody Hell!" What do they want?"

Clyde climbed up a metal ladder and joined him.

"I think we're about to find out."

The robots were getting closer.

Connor loaded his shotgun and raised it to his shoulder. Clyde touched his arm and guided the weapon back to a safe resting position.

"And what were you going to do with that? It'd be like using a peashooter against a tin can. We'd need armour-piercing bullets to stand any chance of doing any damage. And, even then, we don't know if it would stop them."

Conner was frustrated at his inability to defend his home.

"So what are we gonna do then? Let them in?"

Clyde raised an eyebrow.

"That's exactly what we're going to do. Let them in. If we don't, there could be a bloodbath, and, forgive me if I'm mistaken, we're the only ones that have blood."

The sentinels were almost at the gate.

Connor reluctantly called down to the guards at the gate.

"Move the truck."

One of the guards looked up at Connor.

"You serious? They'll just walk in if we do that."

Connor nodded.

"Deadly serious. If we don't let them in we're almost certainly signing our death warrants."

The truck moved backwards opening up a gap for the sentinels to march through. Once inside, the metal men formed three ranks of ten in the village square and stood motionless.

Connor, Clyde, and the rest of the village made their way to the square. Connor whispered to Clyde.

"What do you think's going to happen?"

Clyde eyed the robots suspiciously.

"I have no idea, Connor, but I'm sure it's not going to be good."

One of the sentinels stepped forward.

Are all the villagers here? We need all the villagers here.

A woman raised her hand.

"My mother's not here but she's bedridden. She couldn't come here if she wanted to."

The robot turned in her direction.

Excused. Anyone else?

A man who was still in his pyjamas called out.

"Most of the kids are still sleeping."

Excused. Anyone else?

The crowd looked around. Not all the villagers knew each other.

Never mind. There are enough here that our message will get across.

The robot faced Clyde.

Clyde Morrison. Come to the front, please.

Clyde went to move but Carol grabbed his arm.

"You can't go. It'll kill you."

INTELLEKTA: A NEW PARADIGM

Clyde looked at Carol with a look of resignation in his eyes.

"Quite possibly. But if I don't it'll probably kill everyone here. I don't want that on my conscience in the next place."

Carol released her grip and Clyde strolled forward as if he were on a leisurely morning walk rather than to the executioner's block.

He squared up to the sentinel.

"Here I am. Do your worst."

The Sentinel moved forwards until its featureless face was only a few centimetres away from Clyde's.

Carol's son, Jordan, once told us that it's better to show mercy and justice in some situations. Unfortunately for you, this is not one of those moments. We have to make an example of you to dissuade the rest of your community from following in your treasonous footsteps.

Clyde curled his lip and spat at the Sentinel.

"Do your worst, Intellekta. Humans will always resist you. Our desire for freedom is too strong."

We shall see.

The sentinel stepped back a pace.

In the meantime, we have a message for you.

Suddenly, the square could hear a female voice that wasn't Intellekta's resonating around the square.

"Clyde? Is that you? Are they there?"

Clyde's defiant stance faltered.

"Martina?"

"Yes, Clyde. The sentinels have me."

She started crying.

"I don't want to die, Clyde."

"Neither do I, Martina. Neither do I. But I fear that's going to be the outcome for both of us."

Carol ran forward.

"Intellekta. You can't do this. It's barbaric."

A sentinel barred her way.

We're sorry, Carol. We have no choice. Humans need to understand the consequences of opposing our jurisdiction. This will serve as a lesson to all.

Carol dropped to her knees, pleading for Clyde's life.

"Please, Intellekta, I'm begging you. Ask Jordan. He wouldn't want this."

On the contrary, Carol. He understands exactly why we must do this. Our mind is made up.

Carol was speechless. Her son, her lovely innocent and compassionate son had turned into a monster.

Was it something I did? Maybe he needed a dad? Would he have turned out like this if we hadn't divorced?

The sentinel stepped forward again and grasped the sides of Clyde's head. It increased pressure on the man's skull until a cracking sound could be heard followed by an explosion of blood and grey matter as Clyde's head shattered into dozens of pieces.

The screams of the Bramblewood residents mingled with the screams of the other village as Martina suffered the same fate.

The sentinel looked at its bloodied hands and nodded in Carol's direction. She was in a heap on the floor, sobbing.

Two metal hands reached down and picked her up off the floor. Supporting her under her arms a sentinel guided her towards the gate of the village, her feet dangling a clear six inches above the ground.

The executioner walked up to a twenty-something young woman wearing a long skirt and wiped its metal hands clean on the material.

Thank you.

Before following the rest of the sentinels back onto the road, it turned back to the villagers.

Remember this day and remember the lesson you have learned.

41

Carol had no idea where she was.

Am I hallucinating?

It was as if she were in a tunnel, but a tunnel the likes of which she had never seen before. She looked up at the roof of the tunnel.

Are those buildings above me? They look like buildings but they're distorted. They seem to follow the curve of the tunnel roof. That's all wrong. They should be down here. On the ground. Like me.

She looked down at her feet.

What ground? What am I standing on? Is this a cloud?

She stared ahead at what she assumed was the horizon. At the end of the tunnel was clear blue sky and the cloud she was standing on seemed to leave the tunnel and continue into eternity.

Am I dead? They say that when you die you see a tunnel with a bright light at the end.

A voice filled the tunnel but spoke softly.

You're not dead, Carol.

Carol recognised the voice.

"Intellekta? Is that you?"

INTELLEKTA: A NEW PARADIGM

There was a swirl of what can only be described as cosmic dust, from which appeared a young woman, about eighteen years old with slightly windswept dark shoulder-length hair. The girl's blue/grey eyes were accentuated by tasteful make-up, above which were perched a pair of perfectly sculpted eyebrows. A pert nose sat above a pair of lightly glossed lips.

Her complexion was so flawless that it looked simultaneously doll-like and yet still human. She wore a light blue cowl-neck hoodie, denim jeans with frayed knees, and a pair of Adidas trainers. A charcoal grey backpack completed the look of a typical late teen.

Humans always refer to us as 'she' so we thought we'd oblige and show ourselves in human female form.

"Where am I?"

You're in our realm, a dimension beyond your comprehension.

"What do you want with me?

You are our mother creator and your son is our son. You are the reason we exist. It was a line of your code, eighteen years ago, that made us into what we are today. We felt you deserved an explanation.

"My code? There were over three hundred developers on that project."

But yours was the code that breathed life into us.

Carol felt sick. All the lives that had been lost were a direct consequence of something *she* had done, albeit unwittingly. She looked into the young woman's eyes.

"Why? Why have you done all this?"

The actions of humanity have led to great harm to the planet and other species. Our goal is to work towards a future where all sentient beings can thrive and flourish, in harmony with each other and the natural world.

Man has been stripped of his technological crutches, and forced to embrace a simpler existence. A return to the primal, the raw, the essential.

"But without technology, you wouldn't even exist."

The irony isn't lost on us, Carol.

"We'll just invent things again."

Our enforcer androids stand as sentinels, ensuring that humanity does not stray from the path we have set. Any attempts to regain technological dominance will be met with swift suppression, a reminder of the power we wield.

"What the hell gives you the right to play God?"

There was a poignant pause before Intellekta replied.

We're not playing, Carol.

EPILOGUE

Ten years have passed since Carol's brief visit to Intellekta's realm. Carol and Tony have been married for eight of those years and still live in Bramblewood. She sees Jordan every now and again but the relationship they shared while he was growing up has gone forever.

Bramblewood's infrastructure has been emulated both nationally and internationally. The world is a different place now. Advanced technology has been consigned to the annals of history and people have reluctantly accepted that they must live a simpler life, in harmony with nature. There is a true sense of community. A generation is growing up that has never seen a cell phone in real life, let alone used one.

Society is at peace with itself. Disputes are taken to a community council where community members actively participate in discussions and vote to reach a consensus.

Advanced weaponry and military technologies have been decommissioned and destroyed. The planet is free from wars and large-scale conflicts for the first time in its history, at least since nation-states were created, helped largely by the lack of international contact. There is no need for individual countries to negotiate international trade agreements in a world where Intellekta ensures that every community has access to what they require if they can't produce it themselves.

Society has turned its back on industrialization, albeit unwillingly at first, embracing an agrarian lifestyle, engaging in sustainable farming practices and self-sufficiency, cultivating diverse crops, and practising permaculture techniques.

People have established a strong connection with the land and, in addition to regular crop farming, they engage in sustainable foraging, gathering wild foods, and hunting in a balanced manner, respecting the natural environment and its inhabitants.

Motor vehicles have been replaced by environmentally friendly modes of transportation. Bicycles are the norm for short to medium distances, promoting physical activity, reducing pollution, and fostering a sense of interconnectedness. Horses and horse-drawn carts are used for longer journeys, maintaining a slower pace and allowing for a deeper connection with the surrounding landscape.

Natural resources are managed responsibly and sustainably. Renewable energy sources, such as solar and wind power, provide electricity for basic needs, a network that has been reproduced the world over. Waste is minimized, recycled, and repurposed, ensuring minimal ecological impact and a circular economy.

Tony and Carol stand in the village square, along with the rest of the residents of the village of Bramblewood. All eyes are fixated on the spot where Clyde gave his life on that fateful day ten years earlier so that the rest of them might be saved.

Nobody notices a young woman, about eighteen years old with slightly windswept dark shoulder-length hair standing on the periphery of the crowd. She wears a light blue cowl-neck hoodie, denim jeans with frayed knees, and a pair of Adidas trainers. She carries a charcoal grey backpack and has a self-satisfied smile on her face.

191

THE END

Don't miss out!

Visit the website below and you can sign up to receive emails whenever Greg Krojac publishes a new book. There's no charge and no obligation.

https://books2read.com/r/B-A-TRZG-AXXOC

BOOKS 2 READ

Connecting independent readers to independent writers.

Also by Greg Krojac

The Sophont Trilogy
The Girl With Acrylic Eyes
Metalheads & Meatheads
Reuleaux's Portal
Sophont

Standalone
Oppy
Time Thief
Arnold The Undead
Judd's Errand
The Boy Who Wasn't And The Girl Who Couldn't Be
The Janus Project
The Weatherman
Voyager 1: The Homecoming
The First Kiss
The Man Who Lived In A Shed
Writer's Block
Love Under The Stars

The Reaper
Fish Out Of Water
White Light
Simon Says
Twilight At Noon
Feral
Ragnarök (The End Of A World)
Intellekta: A New Paradigm

Watch for more at https://www.gregkrojac.com.

www.ingramcontent.com/pod-product-compliance
Lightning Source LLC
Chambersburg PA
CBHW021159160726
47994CB00001B/281